JAN 2011

W

THE DETOUR

THE DETOUR

•

Rosemarie Naramore

AVALON BOOKS
NEW YORK

Published by Avalon Books,
an imprint of Thomas Bouregy & Co., Inc.
160 Madison Avenue, New York, NY 10016

Library of Congress Cataloging-in-Publication Data

Naramore, Rosemarie.
    The detour / Rosemarie Naramore.
        p. cm.
    ISBN 978-0-8034-7703-2 (acid-free paper)   1. City and town
life—Oregon—Fiction.   I. Title.
    PS3614.A685D47 2010
    813'.6—dc22

                                                2010022425

PRINTED IN THE UNITED STATES OF AMERICA
ON ACID-FREE PAPER
BY HADDON CRAFTSMEN, BLOOMSBURG, PENNSYLVANIA

For Mom.
I can't give you a recliner with an ocean view,
but I can give you this book—with all my love.

Chapter One

Paige Kelley stretched her cramped muscles, attempting to loosen them up after a multi-hour road trip from San Diego to the Oregon coast. As much as she hated to take a break from driving, her body needed a respite from the cramped conditions in her economy car. Besides, she needed a moment to gather her thoughts. On the one hand, she was eager to reach her destination, but on the other, she was terrified about what she might find when she got there.

For now, she watched as the water pounded the surf, a kaleidoscope of blue and gray hues enlivening each curling, clawing wave. If she thought the sight would soothe her, she was wrong. This beach along the Oregon coast only vaguely reminded her of home in San Diego. Back home, the waves didn't appear quite as angry as these, and the soft sand felt warm beneath her feet.

It was May, after all. Shouldn't the sands have warmed up by now? But then, Paige remembered that the weather here was often temperamental, quick to turn, courtesy of shifting weather patterns off the coastline.

Here, unlike home, Paige didn't feel the slightest inclination to shed her shoes and run headlong through the sand toward the waves. Maybe if she were still sixteen—young and in love—with Wyatt at her side, his warm hand engulfing her own, she would feel differently.

She smiled at the memory—Wyatt and her running into the frigid water, unconcerned about logs, riptides, sneaker waves, or even outside temperatures. Paige shook her head to ward off the thoughts. It was ancient history—the past, and better left there.

Perhaps there was a storm on the horizon, she mused, shielding her eyes against the pelting sand. The sky *was* an ugly gray, the wind gusts fierce. Or perhaps these waves matched the intensity of her thoughts in some sort of kindred, cosmic connection.

Please come. The words came to mind again, as they had during much of her journey. Even the breaking waves seemed to call out, "Please come." Thinking of those two words caused Paige's heart to give an erratic thump. She saw them in her mind's eye, on the computer screen in an e-mail from her grandmother only days before.

Was Gram ill? It was the only logical conclusion she could draw from the cryptic e-mail. Of course Paige had fired off a quick reply, practically begging her grandmother for answers as to why she needed her to come, but none was forthcoming. She'd attempted to reach her grandmother by phone, but again, to no avail. She'd even attempted to reach a friend of her grandmother's, but had had no luck.

The lack of response only frightened her further—terrified her, actually. Was her grandmother in the hospital? And if so, where? There wasn't a hospital in Agate Cove, but only a medical clinic. Had her grandmother been taken to Portland? Was she alone in a hospital room, with no family nearby? If only she had some answers.

Paige felt a shiver travel down her spine. She simply couldn't lose her grandmother—the grandmother she had only known during the last twelve of her twenty-eight years. Like her step-father Don, her grandmother was her anchor—a kindred spirit who offered unconditional love.

With a sigh, Paige turned away from the ocean.

Never turn your back on the ocean. Don's words of warning sounded in her ears, but then she smiled sheepishly. She was yards away from the shoreline, standing back on a rise and overlooking the thunderous waves. Surely they couldn't reach her up here, unless of course the Oregon coast was struck by a tsunami—and then, well, who knew? She'd seen the tsunami warning signs all along the highway.

Paige sucked in a final, deep, lung-inflating mouthful of sea air and then trudged back up the narrow trail to the parking lot. At her car, she glanced at her watch. It was nearing noon and she was only fifteen miles or so south of Lincoln City. She decided she would grab lunch at a drive-thru there, before continuing on to her grandmother's house at Agate Cove.

Since she hadn't taken time to eat breakfast, her empty stomach rumbled for food, and she feared she might become light-headed without nourishment. She tried to remember. Had she eaten dinner the evening before?

Back in her car, driving Highway 101 along the Pacific Ocean, her thoughts transported her to her first introduction to the Oregon coast some twelve years before. She had accompanied her mother, Eva, on the trip to Oregon, believing the two were finally taking a long-anticipated mother-daughter trip together. Don had encouraged the trip, hoping his wife and daughter might somehow find common ground and mend what had become a strained relationship. But it wasn't to be . . .

Her mother had stopped the car at a beach much like the

one she had left earlier. As both stood overlooking the crash-ing waves, wiggling their shoeless toes in the cold sand, her mother had explained the real reason for the trip—she was leaving Don for another man. Her new love interest was wait-ing in Portland, where the two intended to fly down to Mexico later that evening.

Paige had been dumbfounded, disappointed, and furious, and had demanded to be taken home. It was then her mother dropped the first of two additional bombs. "Your stepfather doesn't want you," she had said succinctly, and at first, Paige hadn't believed her. But then, why had Don let her mother take her away if he wanted her to continue living with him?

And then her mother had given her the next big shock of her life. Paige had a grandmother nearby—a grandmother she would be staying with while her mother went to Mexico. Paige had been stunned. Why had her mother kept her grandmother a secret all those years?

The pain of her stepfather's rejection had sliced through her soul, though she later learned her mother had lied in order to gain her cooperation. Don was readying wanted her to leave— had had no idea that as he was readying for a business trip, his wife was making preparations of her own—and that those preparations had nothing to do with a mother-daughter trip. Don had returned to an empty house and unanswered ques-tions.

Eva knew full well Paige wouldn't have left the only father she had ever known had she not lied to her. Paige felt the sting of her mother's betrayal as if it had happened yesterday, and she attempted to force away the feelings. As a sixteen-year-old, believing her father no longer wanted her in his life, she had felt devastated, and were it not for the love of her grand-mother, she wasn't sure she could have withstood her step-father's supposed rejection during that long summer on the coast.

Fortunately, upon returning from his business trip and finding his wife and daughter gone, Don had embarked upon a search for both and had successfully located Paige by summer's end. She had returned home with him, but Paige had visited her grandmother many summers since—until grown-up responsibilities had limited her free time during the summer.

Her thoughts on the past, Paige sped past a sign without clearly seeing it, and after navigating a series of treacherous curves over several miles, she suddenly hit the breaks. A road crew spread out before her, decked out in neon orange, apparently working to repair the badly damaged roadway ahead. Fortunately, Paige managed to stop short of what she noticed with horror was a gaping hole in the road. The asphalt came to a jagged end and then dropped away. Had she not successfully applied her brakes, she could have careened over a cliff and into the ocean, and might have taken an unsuspecting road worker or two with her.

Paige rolled down her window in order to call out a shaky apology.

Although the workers glowered at her, it was the scowling deputy that caught her attention. He was some distance away, across the divide, but began striding toward her, stopping just short of the drop-off. "Didn't you see the detour sign?" he shouted. "You could have killed somebody." He shook his head in disgust. "Tourists!"

"I didn't . . ." Paige's words trailed off. That deputy—she knew that voice, or thought she did. It was deeper than she remembered, but when she met his eyes, there was no denying it—the deputy was Wyatt. He was now older, broader, and angrier—but it was definitely Wyatt Hall.

Paige quickly averted her gaze, but too late. She was certain she saw recognition in his ocean blue eyes. She dropped her head, but then turned slightly to wince apologetically at a road worker who approached. She offered a heartfelt apology and braced for the tongue-lashing she deserved. To her surprise, his countenance appeared to soften, and he began directing her on how best to turn the car around. She was soon turned the opposite direction.

The road worker leaned in the open window. "Visiting the coast, are you?"

She attempted a smile. "Actually, I'm on my way to visit my grandmother in Agate Cove."

"Anyone I might know? I live in Agate Cove."

"Mary Mays—do you know her?"

The man smiled broadly, his blue eyes beaming against a ruddy, weathered complexion. "I know her well. It was a real shame about her accident."

Paige opened her mouth to speak, but her voice lodged in her throat. She swallowed hard, staving off panic. "What . . . about . . . her accident?"

"Oh, you don't know?"

Suddenly, Paige heard the sound of a blaring horn, and then watched in abject terror as another vehicle rounded the bend and very nearly plowed into her, before turning the wheel and coming to a stop against the earthen embankment beside the road.

"Ah, heck!" the road worker said. "Here we go again. You'll need to get a move on. Watch for the sign. The detour is about three miles back."

Paige watched him jog over to the other motorist and then glanced in her rearview mirror. Wyatt remained at the edge of the gaping hole, hands on hips, watching her through narrowed eyes.

She considered leaving her vehicle and asking him about her grandmother. Maybe he knew something if he worked in the area. She could easily call out to him across the divide, but she couldn't decide if it was a good idea or not. He looked so angry.

Just as she was about to climb out of the car to speak to

Wyatt, she heard the rap of knuckles against her passenger-side window. She glanced up to see another road worker waving her off.

Resignedly, she drove away, attempting to steady her pounding heart as she focused on the road ahead. She'd just experienced two shocks to her system: seeing Wyatt Hall again after all these years, and learning that her grandmother had had an accident. She prayed her grandmother was all right, and that the detour was a short one so she could get to her soon.

Her thoughts turned to Wyatt. He was the last person she had expected to see. Since he was wearing a law enforcement uniform, she reasoned he must be working in the area. Hadn't her grandmother mentioned he was working for Homeland Security, with Washington, D.C. as a base of operations? She couldn't help wondering what had brought him back to Agate Cove, but then, he had always loved the ocean. She remembered his parents had a cottage several miles south of town that they visited religiously each summer.

Paige found herself wishing she could keep her thoughts on the matter at hand—the detour—rather than on Wyatt. She very nearly missed the sign a second time, but managed to break to a near stop in order to turn left. She turned and then pulled over onto the shoulder of the narrow roadway in order to study the sign.

She wondered, how could she have missed the bright orange sign? Her eyes widened as she studied it. The forced detour wasn't what she expected—a short jog around the damaged roadway. Instead, another sign depicted a map directing motorists along a fifty-mile stretch to Interstate 5, at which time, in order to reach Agate Cove, she would need to head two miles north on I-5, exit the freeway, and then take another route approximately fifty-five miles back to Highway 101—distance of detour: over one hundred miles.

Paige groaned aloud. She should have parked her car and

taken a running leap over the hole in the road! She could have walked to her grandmother's. If only she had flown to Portland as her stepfather had suggested. She could have rented a car and taken a different route to Agate Cove altogether. But she hated to leave her car behind, since she knew she would need it during her visit. The prospect of driving her grandmother's lumbering one-ton truck wasn't particularly appealing.

Attempting to keep calm and focused, she reached for her cell phone and punched in her grandmother's phone number. No one answered, nor did an answering machine offer an opportunity to leave a message. "Gram," she moaned, "pick up—*please.*"

She dialed her stepfather next. He picked up on the second ring. "Paige, have you arrived already?" he asked.

"No, Dad," she said with a sigh. "Turns out there's damage to Highway 101—the road's practically gone at one point . . ."

"What are you going to do, Paige?" he cut in. "Is it safe? Maybe you should come home."

"I'm currently about to take a very lengthy detour. And I'm worried sick about Gram. I spoke to a road worker who told me she's had an accident, but I wasn't able to find out any details."

Don sighed loudly. "Paige, try not to worry. I'm sure she's fine. If it was too serious, I know one of Mary's friends would have tried to reach you."

"I hope you're right. I really do."

"Paige, really, try not to worry. It won't do any good. You need to keep your mind on your driving."

"I know," she conceded.

"I can fly out if you need me. I can take the first flight out to Portland."

"No, no you can't, but I love you for offering."

"You know I will . . ."

"Dad, we can't risk losing the Lawton Account. They're counting on us. It's bad enough I've left you in the lurch."

"You haven't left me in the lurch," he assured her. "Your ol' dad is up to speed, thanks to you. I expect the presentation will go just fine, although I admit I don't have your finesse when it comes to handling clients."

"Hey, Dad, I learned from the best—remember?"

"Right. Me." Don chuckled. The truth was, her stepfather was the best public relations man in Southern California and had taught her everything she knew. As director of PR at her stepfather's firm, she had excelled under his tutelage.

"Paige, just don't worry about things here. And I mean it. If you need me, call, okay?"

"I will," she told him, ending the call and starting the long drive ahead.

As she drove, Paige suddenly wished Don *was* with her. His steady presence had been the stabilizing force in her life when her mother had provided anything but stability. Don had married Eva when Paige was a toddler, and had raised her as if she were his own child. He couldn't have been a better father.

Sometimes she wondered if nurture had more to do with a child's development than nature, since she was much more like her stepfather than her mother, both in temperament and personality. She decided to ponder the question later, however, and instead turned on the radio, hoping the soft music might calm her mind. Unfortunately, it only made her sleepy, and she turned it off.

Finally, genuinely afraid she might fall asleep, Paige pulled into a rest area to freshen up. She left her car and headed into the cinderblock structure, where she promptly tossed icy cold water in her face. She glanced up at her reflection in the mirror

above the sink and watched the water slide down her cheek-
bones and then drip down her chin.

Staring into her own eyes, she was struck once again by
how much she resembled her grandmother: same auburn hair,
same green eyes and long, dark lashes, same full lips—she'd
even inherited her petite frame from Mary.

Paige finished up in the restroom and headed to her car. A
half hour later she saw a sign indicating that Interstate 5 was
just ahead, and she followed the directions to the major highway. She drove north a couple of miles, watchful of any and
all signs, and soon spied the exit she was seeking. Within moments, she found herself back on a narrow road that, according to another large sign, twisted and turned all the way back
to Highway 101.

Well on her way now, Paige felt relief that she didn't suffer
from car sickness, since this particular road proved to be a
veritable roller coaster of driving thrills and chills. When she
finally arrived at Highway 101, she halted at a stop sign and
glanced to her left. She saw the big gaping hole again—only a
short distance away. From this side, it appeared even more
ominous, since road workers had yet to clear away a pile of
fallen trees, some with pointed tops and others with root sys-
tems, aimed toward the ocean below.

Paige eased onto the roadway, and then watched carefully for
the turn to her grandmother's home. She was afraid that if she
blinked, she might miss it. Suddenly, she spotted the turn and
went left down a narrow, sandy lane. Scraggly trees grew all
around and some slapped the sides of the car as she drove along
the road that veered to the left, just as it appeared the road might
drop into the ocean.

She drove for about a quarter mile, precariously close to a
cliff's edge on her right. When the little lane suddenly dipped
and she couldn't see land beyond the nose of her car, she nearly
cried out in terror. To her immense relief, the car dropped safely

onto the lane. She didn't remember that particular feature of the road from her youth.

Paige did remember the magnificence of the breathtaking ocean view to her right, from her vantage point a couple hundred feet above the crashing waves. She had forgotten just how high her grandmother's home sat above the ocean. She felt relief that it was still light outside, since she wasn't certain she could have successfully maneuvered the lane under the canopy of night.

Soon the lane angled upward and she climbed again. The vegetation around the lane grew thicker before the car suddenly burst into a grassy clearing. Paige gasped. Her grandmother's home was so striking, it never failed to take her breath away. The massive stone home towered above her, so weathered and beautiful it appeared to have been carved from the very cliff it was built upon. An unattached garage, a new addition to the home since her last visit, was architecturally similar to the home, and boasted what appeared to be an apartment that extended the length of the three-car garage. A clutch of pines behind the home provided a lush, green backdrop to an already picture-perfect scene. Paige steered along the circular drive in front of the house and parked.

She climbed out of the car, surprised by the gust of wind that struck her and nearly sent her tumbling onto her backside. She'd forgotten how windy it could get atop the cliff. She braced against it, tugged her jacket around her, and dashed to the front door. She rang the bell, but apparently her grandmother wasn't home.

Paige glanced around, wondering what to do next. Should she drive into town and attempt to obtain answers from some of her grandmother's friends? She knew Mary was very close to Jeanette, the owner of the diner on Main Street. Or she could check with Dori, who owned the souvenir shop nearby the convenience store, or perhaps Minnie, who owned the local bed-and-breakfast, might have answers.

She decided to stay put for the time being. Hopefully her grandmother would be home soon.

Paige hugged herself against the cold, and then turned to survey her surroundings. For lack of something constructive to do, she headed across the front lawn. It was the shape of an irregular half circle and spread out before her like a lush, green carpet. She wondered if her grandmother tended the beautifully maintained patch, or if she had hired landscapers.

From the linear patterns crisscrossing the earth, she deduced it had been mowed recently. She felt a persistent itching in her nose. She was allergic to grass, which was why Don had pulled up all the sod on the minuscule lot of his San Diego home and landscaped with rock and other hypoallergenic and non-offensive materials. It was Don who had driven her to her childhood allergy appointments, who had attended every school play and every dance recital. It was Don who had parented her, while Eva had spent the bulk of her time at her health club, sculpting her already-perfect body.

Paige shook off thoughts of her mother, physically moving her head from side to side. She didn't want to think about her mother now.

She reached the end of the lawn. Were it not for the low fence that cordoned off the area, she could have taken one more step and plunged over the side of the cliff. She reached a tentative hand toward the fence, relieved to find it sturdy. She wondered why her grandmother had replaced the taller fence she remembered, since this fence was so short, one *could* easily topple over it and into the churning ocean below.

She glanced around and saw the fence ran the length of the semicircle. Cautiously, she peered over the drop-off, felt a wave of dizziness, and pulled back with a gasp. *Wow, she was high up here.* Somehow, she expected the drop-off wouldn't feel as high as it once had, now that she was grown.

She couldn't help but wonder again why her grandmother hadn't installed a more substantial barrier, but then she realized that a taller fence would block out much of the view. And the view was glorious.

From a safer vantage point, Paige surveyed the ocean. It was mid-afternoon now, and overcast, but suddenly, a beam of sunlight burst through the lone, puffy white cloud among the gray clouds in the sky. The effect was dazzling, as if she'd been watching a black-and-white movie and somebody had flipped on the color switch. Paige moved closer to the low fence, as if pulled by an invisible string, and stared at the ocean. The color of the ocean under that beam of light was so beautiful, like a blue gem with striations of aqua through it, that she wanted to touch it. She finally pulled her eyes to the base of the rugged cliff and watched the waves pound the rocky surf, one after the other, the same yet different each time.

In San Diego, she had an ocean view from her condo, but nothing like this. There she was blocks away from the ocean on a low hillside with neighbors above, beside, and below. But she *could* see the ocean. It was like an old friend, always there, but rarely demanding anything of her other than an occasional glance. She couldn't even recall the last time she had visited the beach. She searched her memory. *Wait,* she had picnicked there with a friend earlier in the month.

When a big gust of wind suddenly slammed into her, she felt herself sway with the strength of it, and decided it was time to put some distance between herself and the cliff. She turned to leave, when suddenly a large hand clamped down on her arm and tugged her away from the fence. She spun away from the shock of it, but the warm hand held firm.

"Paige!" cried a voice—a familiar voice.

It took several seconds for her to register Wyatt's face, inches from her own, since wind-whipped hair slashed across her face, obscuring her view of him. She started when a gentle hand smoothed the windblown hair off her face and held it back for her.

"Are you all right?" he said, attempting to speak above the wind gusts. "You nearly went sailing over that fence!" He shot the low fence an angry glance, as if it was the fence's fault.

"I'm fine," she said, watching him with unconcealed surprise. She was sure she had seen anger on his face earlier at the damaged roadway. She'd definitely heard it in his voice. But now she detected nothing but concern.

He smiled, his eyes seeming to pass over her face. "It's always a good idea to stand back from that fence, but especially when it's windy. Sometimes the wind hits you so hard it knocks you off balance."

She only nodded in response, still watching him curiously. Her eyes passed over his face this time, taking in the crisp blue eyes, straight nose, and strong chin with a cleft. Wyatt had definitely grown up.

Suddenly, he grinned ruefully. "You very nearly had your second near-death experience today."

"What? Oh. Yes," she said with an apologetic wince. "I missed the detour sign and barely missed the road workers. I'm really sorry."

"Well, you weren't the first, and you won't be the last," he said, still trying to speak above the noise of the gusty winds that slapped against his jacket.

When he reached for her hand and led her across the lawn toward the house, she took the opportunity to gather her wits and thoughts. *Gram!* she thought. She came to an abrupt stop, and Wyatt paused to watch her curiously.

"Where's my grandmother? And what are you doing here?"

He gave her a puzzled glance. "She's in town visiting a friend—at least, that's the story she gave me. And . . . I live here."

Chapter Two

I should clarify," Wyatt said with a grin. "I'm living here for the time being."

The two were in the great room in the garage apartment. Paige stood in front of the picture window, admiring the view, but turned back to him. "But Gram is all right? You're sure?"

"She's fit as a fiddle, other than the foot. She broke it four days ago."

"How did she do that?"

"Well, that's the tricky part. She won't tell me. She said something about twisting it while walking on the beach, but near as I can tell, she broke it sometime during the night, because I had seen her around ten o'clock Monday evening, as I was getting home from a double shift, and she was walking fine then. The next morning, she was limping and asked me to drive her to the clinic. So it wasn't likely she broke it on the beach. I've given up trying to get a straight answer from her. The truth is, your grandma is behaving awfully strange these days."

"You don't think . . . ?"

"No, no," he said with a reassuring smile, waving off her fears that Mary might be experiencing the early stages of dementia. "Absolutely not—her mind is as sharp as ever, but"—he shrugged—"she is up to something."

Paige shook her head, attempting to process. "And why is it you're living here . . . for the time being?" Paige glanced around at the apartment. "Why did Gram have this built—for you?"

He laughed. "No, it's not for me. She said something about getting on in years and maybe eventually needing live-in help around the place. I'm here, because—you saw the condition of 101 just south of here—well, my house is south of there, south of that big, gaping hole in the road. It doesn't make sense for me to drive the detour multiple times a day in order to do my job, so . . ."

"And your job is?" she cut in.

Wyatt shook his head in surprise. "So Mary didn't mention me, or my living here, or my new job to you?"

"No." Paige realized that her grandmother had been uncharacteristically tight-lipped. She wondered if she had divulged anything about her life to Wyatt.

"I'm undersheriff," Wyatt told her, answering her questions. "Sheriff Hughes offered me the job six months ago, and . . . I took it."

"So you're living here, and Sheriff Hughes is living . . ."

"Where he's always lived—also south of here. When law enforcement is needed south of the big, gaping hole, he takes the call, and I handle—"

"Everything north of the big, gaping hole," she said, understanding dawning.

"Well, not everything, since"—he grinned ruefully—"since, thanks to an awfully rainy, rainy season and a subsequent landslide, we have another big, gaping hole twenty miles north of Agate Cove."

"You mean . . . we're sort of . . . trapped here?"

He laughed. "Well, no—we do have our handy, dandy detour, but, well . . . I suppose we are sort of an island unto ourselves these days."

"So, who handles law enforcement issues north of the other big, gaping hole?" she quizzed.

"That would be Deputy Banks."

"Does he live north of that hole?"

"No—like me, he's relying on the kindness of another county resident. He's living in a basement somewhere. Personally, I haven't seen his digs, since I'm not inclined to make what amounts to an even longer detour than you drove in order to check it out."

Paige sighed. "Wow."

"Yeah, life is mighty complicated around here, in light of that . . ."

"That hundred-mile-plus detour," she said dismally, and then her voice rose. "Wyatt, Agate Cove relies on its summer tourist industry to stay afloat during the off-season. How will the town survive if tourists don't come? I mean, I drove that detour, and it's a lot to ask of anyone, even if you're coming from I-5 to begin with."

Wyatt sighed loudly. "Therein lies the question we've all been asking. Without tourists coming this summer season, I'm not sure how the town will manage to survive. Would you like a bottle of water or a soda?"

Wyatt's shift in conversation took Paige by surprise. "Uh, yeah, a soda would be great."

Wyatt left the room and Paige heard the tinkle of ice in a glass and the snap of the pop top. She glanced toward the kitchen, where Wyatt stood with his back to her, pouring soda into a glass. When he bent to grab a dish towel he had dropped on the floor, she watched the play of muscles in his broad, muscular back. He picked up the glass of soda, but briefly put it down on a small tabletop in order to shed his duty belt and drape it onto the back of a chair. Since he was turned toward her now, she noted the crisp crease in his tan slacks—a polyester blend that emphasized his powerful, well-muscled thighs.

Wyatt had always been a handsome young man, but now, at thirty-one, the word *handsome* didn't adequately describe his good looks.

Paige gulped when he caught her staring at him. Her cheeks flamed red, while his face remained impassive as he crossed the room and passed the soda to her, and then indicated the sofa with a nod of his head.

She sat down and wrapped both hands around the frosty glass. It was good to sit. It gave her an opportunity to let the good news sink in. Her grandmother had a broken foot but was otherwise okay. In her worried mind, she had conjured up far worse. She raised the frosty glass to cool her warm cheeks.

"You were terrified, weren't you?" he said, interrupting her thoughts. "You were worried sick about Mary. It's probably why you missed those detour signs earlier."

"Well, to be honest, I was. Gram sent me an e-mail asking me to come, but didn't tell me anything else. She didn't mention the foot . . ." She shook her head. "I've called and called, but she never answers my calls. I haven't been able to leave a message, since the machine is apparently turned off."

"She's rarely home," Wyatt supplied.

"Why did she ask me to come?" Paige mused. "Not that I mind," she added quickly. "I'm glad to come." She furrowed her brow in thought. "Maybe she needs help getting around."

Wyatt shook his head. "Nope, I'm at her disposal. Since I spend the bulk of my time tooling around the twenty-five miles or so between the holes in the road, I'm always a phone call away." He stroked his chin thoughtfully. "No, she called you here for something else—something she doesn't want me to know."

Paige shook her head ruefully. "Could it be you're being a tad suspicious? Maybe she just wanted to see me."

"Mary would never pull you away from your life and your job if she didn't have a good reason. I know that much after having lived here the past month or so."

"Well, you're right about that."

A companionable silence ensued as Paige searched her brain for answers. When she found none, her thoughts turned back to Wyatt, who was now sitting in a nearby recliner with his feet propped up, watching her face.

"You look good," he said finally, cocking his head to the side.

Paige reddened under his scrutiny. "You do too."

"It's been, what—ten years?"

She searched her memory. "Yes. Ten years. Remember . . ."

Wyatt suddenly smiled without mirth. "Yeah, I remember." He lowered the leg rest of the recliner and stood up. "I'm going to change out of this uniform."

He was gone all of two minutes, and returned wearing well-worn jeans, a T-shirt with the local high school mascot emblazoned across the front, and slippers. "It's been a long day," he said, as he dropped back into the recliner. "With tourists intent on jumping the hole all day, it's a miracle nobody's dead, and . . . I'm beat."

"I can leave," she offered, beginning to rise from the couch. "I can wait in my car."

"Right, like I'm going to let you sit out there in your car. You're fine here," he assured her.

Paige was silent for a moment, thinking about the detour sign she had missed. Apparently it was a regular occurrence. She leaned forward in her seat and caught Wyatt's gaze. "Maybe you should post additional signs on the road," she said, her brows furrowed in a frown. "You know, perhaps give more warning about the upcoming road collapse. Maybe signs at different intervals would better alert drivers to the oncoming detour. If the existing sign isn't working . . ."

"Why didn't we think of that?" Wyatt said, and Paige wasn't

sure if he was serious or joking. "No, really, why didn't we think of that?" he said with a self-deprecating laugh. "Good idea—we'll put up more signs—well, either that or a ramp for the really preoccupied driver—you know, so he or she has a fighting chance."

Paige chuckled, but then a silence ensued again, and this time it wasn't so comfortable. Paige suspected she had caused the awkwardness by referencing their last meeting, before he had left town to ready for college. The two had met on the private beach just below her grandmother's house. The pristine beach had been in her grandmother's family for a hundred years.

There, beside an unusually calm ocean, Wyatt had taken her in his arms, declared his love for her, and asked her to marry him. And in truth, she had loved him too.

Don would have been devastated if his daughter, a girl with so much promise and potential, had thrown away a bright future by marrying while still a teenager. Paige knew then, and now, it would have killed him. It was a mistake her mother had made—a mistake that had cost many people dearly.

That day on the beach, Wyatt had pulled a ring from his jacket pocket and attempted to put it on her finger. She had pushed him away. She'd tried to explain her reasons, suggested that if their love was true, it would survive time and distance. It hadn't.

Paige suspected the blow to his young man's ego had been too much, and as Don had suggested would happen when she had confided in him upon arriving home, Wyatt had seemingly forgotten all about her as he completed college and embarked upon a law enforcement career.

"Are you married?"

The question took Paige by surprise, pulling her from thoughts apparently in sync with his.

"Uh, no, I'm not. My work keeps me busy."

He nodded. "Seems we've both taken a similar road—

career . . . and . . . all that." He rose again from the recliner, and this time strode to the fridge and grabbed a soda for himself. He didn't bother with a glass. He returned to the chair, opened the can, and took a long, slow sip.

"What prompted you to give up your job in Washington?" Paige asked.

"Your grandma told you about that?"

"Well, no—I mean, I knew you were working in Washington, but now you're here . . ." She spread her hands.

"I've always loved the ocean," he said, avoiding the question. Paige noticed. She sensed he didn't want to talk about his previous job. And she knew it was true, that he loved the ocean. Although his parents spent summers in Agate Cove, she remembered him expressing a desire to live there year-round. She remembered him talking about captaining a fishing boat, or giving whale watching tours.

He suddenly shifted the conversation away from himself and to her. "Mary tells me you're doing PR for your stepdad's firm?"

She nodded. "Since college. I love it. It turns out . . ."

"You're good at it." It was a statement, not a question. "You were always . . . smart."

She smiled at the compliment, and then checked her watch—anything to avoid meeting his crisp blue eyes. They were like a reflective pool, sometimes smooth and serene, at ease, and at other times tumultuous like the ocean. If the eyes were the window to the soul, then Wyatt's eyes were akin to a picture window. And oh, how she had stared into those eyes.

She remembered the first time he had really looked into *her* eyes. She had been sixteen. It was her first summer with her grandmother. She was still reeling from the shock of her mother's betrayal, of her supposed abandonment by her stepfather, and the discovery that she had a grandmother. She had initially walked around Agate Cove like a zombie, with her thick, dark hair tumbled forward like a curtain across her face—an attempt to hide her pain from probing eyes.

One day she had been sitting ocean side. It was a calm day on the beach, and she had been propped against a log, staring out at the waves. She hadn't noticed the boy nearby, staring at her.

When he had ambled over to her, his handsome face bespeaking his curiosity, she had been anything but courteous to him. She had ignored his questions, had even shooed him away with a frustrated hand. But he had sat down anyway and begun talking.

It was like that for several days. She had pretended she wanted him to go away, but oddly, she'd returned to the same spot on the beach day after day, and each time, he'd returned as well.

Soon, she'd found her defenses crumbling, as he'd spoken openly about his life—about conflicts with his father, and about his fears for the future.

Until that summer, Paige hadn't ever been so bold as to even speak to a boy, but with Wyatt, she had found herself opening up to him—divulging her story. He had been kind and sympathetic. And then one day, he had reached a gentle hand to her face, pulled back her hair, and removed the thick glasses she wore.

She would never forget the way his eyes had widened. "You're beautiful," he'd told her. When he'd gently put her glasses back on her face, he had grinned. "You're a knockout. Let's let that be our secret."

The next summer, she'd returned with contacts, worn her hair in a modern, layered cut, and the cat was decidedly out of the bag. She smiled at the memories. Wyatt had seen her beauty when others hadn't . . .

"What are you smiling about?" His deep voice penetrated her reverie.

She forced the memory away with a shake of her head. "It's nothing. I was just wondering when Gram is going to get home."

"No telling," he said. "And I'm telling you, she's up to something. You want to run into town and grab something to eat? I'll bet you're hungry. The detour alone can work up an appetite in anyone."

"I don't know," Paige said uncertainly. "What if I leave and she comes home?"

"Wait—why didn't I think of it?" he muttered. "I have her cell phone number somewhere around here. Don't know why I didn't store it in my phone . . ."

"Gram has a cell phone now?" Paige said with surprise.

Wyatt nodded. "Yeah, she picked one up recently. She said something about needing it now . . ." He rose and strode to the kitchen. She followed and put the glass in the sink, and watched as he tugged a slip of paper off the fridge. She listened as he dialed Mary.

"Hey, where are you?" he asked in a mock, gruff voice. Paige watched his mouth twitch into a smile. "Well, save us a seat. Paige and I will meet you there."

He was quiet for a second or two. "Yep, she just arrived."

Paige watched Wyatt as he listened to her grandmother, a smile still creasing his handsome face. "She's been worried sick about you, Mary," he scolded. "You ought to be ashamed of yourself." He was silent for a long moment and then laughed. "We'll see you in ten."

He flipped his phone closed. "She's at the diner having dinner with friends. She said she'll wait for us there."

Paige sighed with relief, since she finally knew how Mary was doing and where she was. But why wasn't her grandmother home, kicked back in a chair, with her broken foot raised on a pillow?

"Ready?" Wyatt asked as he sat to pull on a pair of tennis

shoes. She nodded and he stood up. She felt his warm hand on her back as they walked out of the apartment. After he locked it up, he asked, "Do you hear much from your mother?"

Paige involuntarily stiffened at the question. "Uh, well, I get the occasional postcard."

"Is she still gallivanting around the globe with that body-builder?"

"Oh, she's still gallivanting, but with a different body-builder."

Perhaps Wyatt detected the pain in her voice, since he gently eased her to a stop by taking her hand. He sought her gaze. "I'm sorry, Paige. I shouldn't have brought her up."

"No, no, it's okay," she assured him. "It's just odd, being back here. I find myself thinking about her. When she brought me here, it effectively marked the end of our . . . relationship."

"Her choice, not yours," Wyatt said crisply.

"It's difficult to explain," she said, glancing off at the ocean, and then turning back, "but it's bittersweet. I lost her, but gained a grandmother . . . and you . . . then."

To her horror, Paige felt tears pool in her eyes. It was ridiculous, and she turned away, embarrassed. When Wyatt turned her toward him and wrapped her in his strong arms, she wasn't sure how to respond. She was mortified by her show of emotion, but more surprising was her response to him. Having his arms around her felt . . . right—as if time had stood still.

Apparently, he felt the same. "You still fit," he whispered.

When she finally pulled away, meeting his face with a tremulous smile, she shook her head. "I'm sorry. I'm being silly."

"You're not. And don't be sorry." He laughed without humor. "Although there are plenty of things I'm sorry about."

She eyed him questioningly.

"I'm sorry I stopped writing."

When they had parted ways all those years ago, he had

promised to write, and he had—for a while. But soon, he'd stopped returning her letters. She had been devastated.

"Why wouldn't you have stopped writing?" she said too brightly. "You were young, with your whole life ahead of you."

"I was an infant," he said with disgust, "a stupid, prideful kid."

"No, Wyatt—you got on with your life. What else could you have done? We were both too young."

Wyatt appeared about to say something, but didn't. Instead, he led her to his truck and opened the passenger-side door. She climbed in and watched him round the front of the cab.

Inside, she belted in, and then neither spoke as Wyatt drove swiftly down the sandy lane. It was obvious he knew it like the back of his hand, but Paige found herself bracing her hand on the door handle. Wyatt noticed.

"Sorry—but if it makes you feel better, I could drive this in my sleep. Heck, I do drive it in my sleep."

"After a long shift," she said with a smile.

He nodded.

"Are you the only law enforcement officer working between the North Hole and the South Hole?" she asked with a grin.

He laughed. "That's good—North Hole and South Hole. From here on out, that's what we'll call them. And in answer to your question, no, I'm not alone. A deputy by the name of Doug Harada works opposite shifts to mine."

"And what shifts do you work?" she asked with interest.

"It varies. Doug has a wife and kids, so I generally pick up the less desirable shifts."

"That's nice of you," she observed.

"Well," he said with a laugh, "I'm a nice guy."

Chapter Three

Despite her broken foot, Mary awkwardly rose from the booth and hobbled toward the restaurant entrance when she spied Paige pass through the front doors. Paige saw her at the same second, and closed the distance between them before her grandmother could take another difficult step.

"I was so worried about you, Gram," Paige said in a rush. "I tried to reach you. Why haven't you been taking calls?"

"I'm sorry, honey. I've been so busy. I didn't mean to worry you. I know I should have called."

"Yes, you should have," Wyatt said sternly, as he strode past the two women and dropped into a chair beside Mary's friend, Jeanette. "Hey, Jeanette," he said to the tall redhead, "since you own this establishment, what's good on the menu?"

"You know full well everything's good on this menu," she told him drolly, shaking her head of unruly curls. "You eat here practically every day, Wyatt."

Wyatt moved his head from side to side, as if weighing her answer. "Well, I had a meatloaf here once that wasn't so . . ."

"Oh, you hush your mouth," she warned.

"Yes, you hush your mouth," Mary said, as she hobbled back to the table with Paige bringing up the rear, a worried frown marring her face.

"Gram, shouldn't you have crutches?" Paige asked with concern.

"Ah, probably," she admitted, "but they slow me down."

"Wouldn't want to do that," Wyatt muttered as he reached for a menu.

Mary raised a threatening fist before awkwardly climbing into the booth. "What did I just tell you, Wyatt? Hush!"

"Do you think I'm worried about your threats?" he taunted. "I can outrun you now."

"I wouldn't bet on it," Mary retaliated.

Paige slid into the booth, both surprised and delighted by the repartee between her grandmother and her former boyfriend. It was clear the two were fond of each other.

"You'd better mind your p's and q's, young man," another nearby voice said. Paige turned to see Minnie, the petite, blond owner of the local bed and breakfast, approach. "Mary's liable to toss you out on your ear."

"Well, if she did, you'd take me in," Wyatt said confidently.

"There's no room at the inn," Minnie said as she sat down at the table. "Besides, I'd charge you rent."

"You don't charge Wyatt rent?" Jeanette asked Mary, aghast.

"We've worked out a bartering arrangement," Wyatt said, arching his brows suggestively. "It's working out very well."

"Right," Mary said in measured tones, shooting Wyatt a look of daggers, "and my lawn has never looked better."

"Oh, that's true," Paige said with a chuckle. "When I pulled up, I wondered who was taking care of the lawn. Looks good, Wy," she said, using the shortened version of his name that she had used when they were young.

He glanced up and met her gaze. A silent communication passed between them, but she couldn't decipher exactly what it meant. To her horror, her cheeks reddened and then practically burst into flames when the three other women at the table began taunting Wyatt. "Looks good, Wy!" they teased.

"Hey, Paige, *Wy* looks pretty good, too, eh?" Minnie laughed. "Hey, if memory serves, didn't you two used to date?"

"Paige, have you had a chance to see Wyatt in his uniform?" Jeanette asked, comically raising her eyebrows. "Wow—you don't want to miss him! With that broad chest and those huge biceps, he's"—she shook her head, as if searching for words—"he's a marvel of human anatomy."

"Practically a god," Minnie confirmed.

"Hmm," Wyatt said noncommittally, "you can tell all that from my uniform?"

"Before the roads collapsed, Wyatt was our town's most notable tourist attraction," Jeanette quipped. "Wyatt hasn't figured out yet that half the women in this town call the station just to have *him* respond to their calls. And just how do you respond, Wyatt?" she teased, with a wicked gleam in her eye.

"I'm not even going to dignify that question with an answer," he said, as he dropped his head and then shook it before studying the menu. "Like a bunch of school girls, or a gaggle of geese," he intoned.

"Don't you mean 'hens'?" Jeanette said.

"Whatever . . . I'm minding my own business over here," Wyatt said, still without lifting his head, but then he glanced up briefly and caught Paige's gaze. "Stay away from them, Paige. They're liable to have a corrupting influence."

"Well, I think I'm insulted," Jeanette said, feigning offense. "Are you trying to say we're a bad influence on the younger generation—three harmless, elderly women like us?"

"Yep," Wyatt said succinctly.

"Who are you calling elderly, Wyatt?" Mary demanded. "I'm not too elderly to take you over my knee."

Wyatt met her gaze, his brows furrowed in a frown. "I . . . didn't call you elderly."

"You'd better watch yourself, young man," Minnie threatened.

Wyatt raised his hands as if warding them off. "Stop—I didn't call anybody elderly. Help me, Paige." He caught her gaze again before glancing down and pretending to study the menu.

"Gram, how'd you hurt your foot?" Paige asked, diverting the conversation from Wyatt. He looked wholly uncomfortable by now.

"Oh, I twisted it when I was walking on the beach."

"Did not," Wyatt said, without looking up.

"What did I tell you, Wyatt?" Mary said tiredly. "Hush!"

"If I hush, do you promise not to evict me?"

Before she could answer him, a waitress appeared to take their order. Just as they were finishing up, another of Mary's friends, Dori, joined the group. The plump brunet arrived at the table breathless and windblown.

"How was business today? Did you sell any souvenirs?" Mary asked hopefully.

Dori sighed as she pulled up a chair and sat down. "Not a one." She noticed Paige then. "Girl, it's *so* good to see you. Thank God you've come." She glanced at Mary again. "Are we ready to talk . . . ?"

Jeanette and Minnie cleared their throats simultaneously, and Mary shot a pointed look at Wyatt, who glanced up in time to see it. Dori's eyes widened in shock when she noticed him. "Well . . . hello, Wyatt . . . I didn't see you there."

He looked skeptical. "How could you miss me, being as I'm a veritable statue of Adonis and all?"

"Now, Wyatt, we didn't say that," Jeanette said sternly. "We'd hate for all this talk to go to your head."

"Oh, well, yeah," he said with a crooked grin. "We wouldn't want *that* to happen." He caught Paige's eyes, and she saw the sparkle of humor in his.

Paige wondered how Dori had missed a six foot two, blond, and blue-eyed man among a group of women, but then, maybe Dori was preoccupied. She looked preoccupied and disheveled. Her friends watched her with a cautious alarm, apparently fearful she might say too much. Paige picked up on the tension, suspecting that Wyatt was right. Her grandmother was up to something—and her friends were likely part of it.

Paige glanced from her grandmother to the faces of the other women, one by one. Wyatt was right. The four friends definitely had a secret.

Wyatt sought Paige's gaze. "See, I told you. Mary's up to something, and these women are clearly her partners in crime."

"We are not!" they said aghast, and in unison.

"I'm a trained law enforcement officer," Wyatt said, comically narrowing his eyes and regarding each woman with exaggerated suspicion. "And I'm going to find out what each and everyone of you is up to." He smiled without mirth. "It's not as if I don't have the time. With 101 cut off by the North and South Holes, there's not much crime happening in our fair town."

"Well, that's definitely one advantage to being shut off from the world," Mary said too brightly, and then cocked her head. "North and South Holes, did you say? I like that."

Wyatt nodded at Paige. "Give Paige the credit. She came up with it. I want a piece of cake."

"That was a strange shift in the conversation," Dori said.

"He does that all the time," Mary said.

"Cake for the beefcake?" Jeanette said with a chuckle. "I thought cops only eat donuts."

Wyatt opened his mouth to speak, but promptly clamped it shut. He stood up and moved to peruse the assortment of cake slices beneath a glass top. Paige was surprised to see his cheeks stained red.

"Dinner before dessert!" Mary called to him.

"I'm not sure I'm staying for dinner," Wyatt said grumpily. "And you're my landlord, not my mother—even if you aren't charging me rent."

"I'm the nearest thing to a mother you have in this town," Mary told him, smiling affectionately at him. "Well, grand-mother," she clarified.

He glanced up with a quick grin. "You're right about that."

"So, Wy," Jeanette called out, "is that girlfriend of yours still driving the ridiculous detour all the way from Lincoln City to Agate Cove to bring you donuts, because, if so, could you ask her to bring a few dozen here? What's a diner without donuts?"

Wyatt glanced at Paige with alarm, and then averted his gaze.

"She's not your lady friend?" Minnie asked in a singsong voice. "Because, Lordy, she clearly has the hots for you, son."

Jeanette let out a gleeful chuckle. "One of the road workers from the . . . 'South Hole' told me that that little lady shows up on the other side of the hole with bags full of donuts and tries to toss them to Wyatt."

"Well, you know how cops are about their donuts," Mary said, smiling.

The women burst into giggles, and Wyatt shifted uncomfortably as he pretended to study the cake slices. He finally glanced up with a sheepish grin. "Hey, she only did it once, and . . . she throws like a girl. The donuts took a tumble into the ocean."

Paige stared at Wyatt's face, surprised at the crimson stains on his cheeks. She smiled softly, but realized she had felt a misplaced pique of jealousy at the mention of Wyatt having a girlfriend. But why wouldn't he? The man was drop-dead gorgeous, and likely the most eligible bachelor in Agate Cove. Of course he had a girlfriend.

Wyatt steered his truck along the sandy lane to Mary's house. Paige sat in the small space between the driver's seat and the passenger seat, occasionally moving her legs so Wyatt could shift the gears. It was nearly dark by now, and Paige marveled at the ease with which he drove the road. She tried not to think about the precarious drop-off to their right.

As if Wyatt sensed her discomfort, she felt his warm hand on hers. He squeezed her hand ever so briefly, and then returned it to the wheel.

Parked back in front of Mary's house, Wyatt hurried around to help the older woman out of the car. "Thanks, hon," she said warmly.

Wyatt turned to help Paige down from the tall cab of the truck, but she had already dropped down easily. Mary turned to both of them. "Why don't you two take a walk on the beach?" she suggested. "I'm going inside to put this foot up for a while."

Paige met her grandmother's gaze, watching her with concern. "I should stay with you," she said, glancing from Mary to Wyatt uncertainly.

"No, no, that's all right. You two go for a walk. Get reacquainted. But . . . if you could be back here by eight-thirty, that would be great, since the girls are coming over. We'd like you to join us, Paige."

"They're up to something," Wyatt murmured under his breath.

Paige felt uncomfortable leaving her grandmother for any length of time, but Mary seemed adamant. "Really, hon—I think I'll take a short nap, and I know Wyatt would like to visit."

"I can always come over at eight-thirty too," he suggested helpfully.

"Girls only," Mary said with a twinkle in her eye.

"Well, that doesn't seem particularly neighborly," Wyatt said in a mock-disappointed voice. "Regardless, I'm going to help you inside, and then if Paige wouldn't mind a short walk on the beach . . ." His words trailed off as he watched Paige expectantly.

Paige acquiesced when her grandmother nodded encouragingly. She took one of her grandmother's elbows while Wyatt took the other, and they helped her into the huge family room. Mary eased into an overstuffed recliner, and Wyatt bent to raise the leg rest. Paige draped a throw blanket over her.

"All right?" she asked.

Mary yawned. "It's perfect. Now, you two take that walk. The wind has finally died down. It's been so long since you've seen your beach, Paige."

Paige followed Wyatt outside, where the two crossed the manicured lawn to the low fence. When Paige moved to stand behind it, Wyatt reached for her hand. She glanced down at their entwined hands and experienced a feeling of déjà vu.

She shook off the feeling. She and Wyatt were no longer kids. They were light years past their teens, and apparently Wyatt had a girlfriend. Paige slipped her hand out of his and took a step back. She crossed the lawn to the side that overlooked the public beach north of her grandmother's property.

Unlike the rocky drop-off at the westernmost end of the property, this side wasn't a sheer, rocky cliff, but instead a steep, sandy hillside that dropped down onto a long beach, accessed from her grandmother's property by a sandy, zigzagging trail.

Paige stared out at the beach below and noticed a lone figure strolling along, periodically bending to pick something up from the sand. She squinted her eyes, trying to discern if there were others enjoying the quarter-mile-long stretch of beach, but she saw no one. Her eyes traveled to a massive sand dune that sliced across the beach. Typically, tourists could be seen climbing that dune, regardless of the season, but this evening, even the dune was clear of adventurous climbers.

"Agate Cove is like a ghost town," Wyatt said sadly from beside her. "I can't remember a time when there wasn't a single soul on that dune." He smiled into her eyes. "Remember all those times we climbed to the top?"

"It was like sitting on the top of the world," Paige remembered.

"I always thought I was going to die before we reached the top," he admitted.

Paige gave him a startled glance. "You did not! You scaled it like a pro, and you weren't even breathing hard when we reached the top."

"I was too."

"I didn't notice," she said, shaking her head ruefully.

"I was trying to impress you. I wasn't about to let you see me gasping for air. Every time I stopped to look out at the view, and directed you to look out, I was sucking in ocean air as if there wasn't enough to fill my lungs. And then all those times you thought I was joking around—you know, when I pretended to be a man lost in the desert with my face down in the sand—well, I was really dying."

"Huh," Paige said, and then turned to cross the lawn to the other side. She stood for a moment, taking in the sight of the private beach. As on the other side, a steep, sloping hillside led to a beach below. Here, the beach line was considerably shorter, and at the far end, a massive, rocky cliff jutted out into the water—a twin to the one the couple currently stood on. The two formations created a cove where, curiously, the waves appeared to come in less fiercely than on the other side. This side was beautiful, the water a striking sea blue against white sand.

"So pretty," Paige said softly.

"Do you feel like a walk?" Wyatt asked. "I'd bet you're tired from all the driving you've done today."

"I would like to go down to Gram's beach."

Wyatt took her hand as they descended the wooden steps that wound down the hillside. "If you use this stairway when I'm not here, you'll want to be really careful," Wyatt cautioned. "It can get awfully slippery, and at night it's difficult to see."

Paige nodded as they continued the climb down. Finally, they reached the last step, and Paige paused to take in the sights. Dusk had settled quicker than she would have liked, and she suspected they should probably get back to the upper property, but she felt a pull to remain on the beach. This place had always felt magical to her—perhaps because it was her ancestral home—or maybe the ocean itself called to her. She couldn't be sure. In San Diego she was close to the ocean, but she didn't feel the pull there that she experienced here.

"Are you cold?" Wyatt asked.

She shook her head. "I'm fine, thanks."

She strode across the sand then, stopping only briefly to tug off her shoes. The sand here felt soft, much softer than it usually did on the public beach. She jogged to the water's edge and dipped a tentative toe into the icy water.

"It's cold!" Wyatt called a warning.

She turned to meet his smiling face. "It feels great. You should try it."

He only shook his head. "Not tonight—it's getting dark. We should probably go back up."

"Can we come back?" The instant she asked the question, she regretted it. Of course she could come back—alone.

Wyatt crossed the few feet between them and shrugged out of his light jacket. He draped it over her shoulders and then met her gaze, still smiling. "Of course we can come back."

Chapter Four

"Gram, are you sure you're feeling up to having visitors? You really should be resting that foot."

"I had a good nap," Mary told her worried granddaughter. "And I am resting my foot. Besides, we have business to attend to, you and I."

"Me?" Paige asked, furrowing her brow.

"Yes, you," Mary said mysteriously, smiling into her granddaughter's puzzled face.

Soon, Mary's three best friends arrived, having carpooled together in Jeanette's minivan. They entered the house, a flurry of excitement, all talking at once, and hurried into the family room.

"Wow, that was a close call at the diner," Minnie observed. "I thought Wyatt was going to arrest us on the spot."

"Oh, don't be melodramatic," Dori said. "He didn't know what I was talking about."

"Dori, you nearly let the cat out of the bag," Jeanette said in an ominous tone. "Can you imagine what Wyatt would have said if he'd gotten wind of our plan?"

"Well, it isn't as if we plan to do anything illegal," Dori said in a surly tone. "Is it, Mary?"

Mary appeared to weigh the question. "To be honest, I don't . . . know. I . . . hope not."

Paige stared at her grandmother with alarm. "Gram, what are you all planning to do? Wyatt told me you're up to something."

Mary raised a conciliatory hand. "It's nothing for you to worry about, Paige."

"What is it?" she prompted, her narrowed eyes fastened on her grandmother's face.

"It's just, well, in light of my injury . . ."

"Yes, Gram?"

"Well, honey, I'll just come out and say it. I need you to be my surrogate in our plan to save the town."

Paige dropped onto the sofa across from her grandmother's recliner. Her friends seated themselves as well. Paige took a deep, steadying breath. What did her grandmother and her friends plan to do? And why would they wonder if their potential actions were illegal? Oh, gosh, she thought, had they already put their plan—whatever it might be—into action?

Mary read the sick expression on Paige's face. "Paige, get that look off your face. We're not doing anything illegal or— well, even if we are, our hearts are in the right place. Agate Cove is going to die, thanks to those . . . those . . . North and South Holes, if we don't do something to save her."

"It's true," Jeanette agreed. "Our summer season is less than two weeks away. We have to bring tourists here. They're the lifeblood of our town. But who in their right minds will drive that blasted detour—even if they're coming off I-5 in the first place—when once they get here, they can't get back out except by the detour?"

"We're cut off from Lincoln City," Dori added, "and every other tourist sight south and north of here as well."

"We're doomed," Minnie added sadly, "unless we can offer something to visitors that will inspire them to see Agate Cove as a *destination*—rather than simply a pass-through on to other sights—because, well, you can't pass through anymore."

Paige glanced at each woman's face. All wore expressions of fear. She well understood. Everything they said was true. Agate Cove could not survive without an influx of tourists, and it wasn't likely the tourists would come. Paige suspected there wasn't anything these ladies could do to bring them here, either.

Paige sighed and smoothed a hand to her hair. She turned to her grandmother, who spoke before she could.

"Paige, you have to help us. Our plan won't work unless we work together. As I said, I can't hold up my part of the plan, since I went and broke my foot . . ."

"I get it," Paige said. "You need me to fill in for you. Wait a minute. How did you break your foot, Gram? You didn't say at dinner."

Mary gave her a sheepish look. "Oh, I was conducting a trial run of our plan."

"Wyatt said you broke it on the beach," Paige interrupted.

"Well, I actually broke it on the lawn, *after* I came back from the beach. I tripped on a piece of driftwood, but . . . Wyatt got me so flustered with his questions, I didn't know what I was saying. He can be so nosy," she added with a swift shake of her head. "Carrying out our plan right under his nose isn't going to be easy."

Paige watched her grandmother with a puzzled frown. "So tell me, what is it you're planning to do—and right under Wyatt's nose, no less?"

Mary's face lit up. "Okay, I was thinking one day about how Agate Cove got its name . . ."

"Go on."

"Well, obviously the town was named for the agates you used to be able to find all over the beaches. Unfortunately, there just aren't that many agates anymore. I don't really know why, but imagine . . ." She paused for emphasis.

"What?" Paige said, bracing for her answer.

"What if the agates came back? What if there were so many agates, people came in droves to find them? What if rock hounds, and schoolchildren, and retired couples couldn't resist all the beautiful agates scattered all over the public beach?"

Paige shook her head, and then moved forward in her seat. "Gram, do you realize how many agates you would need in order to draw people in numbers?"

"Oh, yes, I think I do."

"Even if you could get your hands on that many agates, how would you get them onto the beach? I mean, the logistics of covering the sand with agates, and managing to do it without being seen, and then keeping the sand covered with agates day after day—I mean, my head is spinning from the magnitude of such a venture." She shook her head to clear it. "Look, it's too huge."

"Then honey, take it one piece at a time. Okay, what did you mention first as a concern? Oh, yes, there's acquiring the agates . . ." Mary's words trailed off as she nodded toward Jeanette, who rose from the sofa and moved to a corner of the room. Paige hadn't noticed a blanket draped over what appeared to be boxes.

"What are those?" Paige asked, frowning.

Jeanette pulled the blanket back with a theatrical flourish. Paige saw boxes and more boxes, but none were marked. "Yeah, so, boxes," she muttered.

"Oh, hold on." Jeanette tugged one open and Paige rose to see the contents. She gasped. The box was filled to the brim with smooth agates of every size, shape, and color.

"Oh, good grief," Paige moaned. "Gram, where did you get those?"

"I bought them off the *Television Shopping Show* that comes on in the middle of the night."

"Okay, I'm not even going to ask you what you've been doing up in the middle of the night, or even how much those agates cost, but Gram . . . it's not enough."

"Which is why we'll buy more," she said reasonably. "They're really not all that expensive, either, since they haven't been professionally polished. They're just stones, but like our town, they're full of the potential to be beautiful. Like Agate Cove, they just need a little polish."

"Bravo!" Jeanette cheered. "Mary, you've always had such a way with words."

"You're an inspiration," Minnie said sincerely.

Paige walked slowly back to the couch and dropped onto the edge. "Look, Gram, how do you know if those are even Oregon Coast agates?"

"I did some research."

"Of course you did," Paige said tiredly, rubbing her eyes. She glanced up. "Okay, so you have several boxes of agates. Tell me, how are we going to get them onto the beach?"

"Easy," Mary said brightly. "We toss them onto the beach— you know, in the same manner as if you're feeding seagulls. And it really shouldn't be that hard, since we'll only really want to distribute them along the wet sand at the water's edge."

"And who's going to do this? I mean, it'll be dark, foggy, and stormy much of the time. How safe will we be walking a quarter-mile stretch of beach?"

Mary cast a worried glance at each of her friends. She realized Paige had a point, but it didn't dissuade her from the plan.

"We're all going to make this work," Mary said eagerly. "Well, you'll be in my place, but the girls will help. We'll have a schedule. You'll each be assigned a night of the week. It'll basically work out so that some of you have agate distributing duty only one day a week, but other weeks, it'll be two. If we all do our parts, no one will get too tired, and we should be able to continue until the roads are repaired by summer's end."

"And what if the roads aren't fixed by then?" Paige asked.

"We'll cross that bridge when we come to it," Mary said confidently.

Paige stood beside her grandmother, in what had been her bedroom during the first summer she had stayed with her and every summer after. Located on the first floor of the home, it was large and painted a soft, seafoam blue, and trimmed in white around the doors and windows. A double bed with a simple white bedspread was centered between two windows, and a dresser was pressed against one wall. The only artwork in the room was a large painting of a lighthouse. Paige had always admired the painting.

"Looks the same," Paige commented to her grandmother, who stood beside her, braced on crutches. Paige had insisted that she use them, once Mary had finally divulged that she had them stored in a closet.

"The room *should* look the same. I haven't changed a thing. Are you tired, honey?"

"My mind and body both are," Paige admitted.

"The girls and I kind of knocked you for a loop with our plan, huh? And seeing Wyatt must have been a bit of a shock."

Paige ignored the comment about Wyatt, true as it was. "You could say your plan threw me for a loop," she said. "Gram, I just don't think it can work. Somebody is bound to see us, and if someone gets wind of the plan, I do think it could mean legal troubles for all of us."

"What do you mean?"

"Well, it seems to me that luring people to the beach using store-bought agates could be . . ."

"Television-bought," Mary corrected her.

"Okay, television-bought agates . . . could be construed as fraud."

"I admit, I have thought about that," Mary said. "But I think we have to take the risk. If we don't, Agate Cove will cease to exist. Minnie is barely managing to keep the bed-and-breakfast open by renting a room to one of the road workers, and Dori's souvenir shop is all but empty every day. Even the diner is suffering, although Jeanette is faring better than most, since the locals do eat there fairly often."

"Gram, I understand what you're saying, and I do want to help, but I just don't know about this particular plan."

Mary appeared to weigh her granddaughter's fears. "Honey, we just don't know what else to do. We have tried other avenues."

"Such as?" Paige prompted.

"Well . . . Dori called the corporate offices at Costco and asked if they would consider opening a store in Agate Cove—because people will drive any distance for a Costco hot dog, but . . . they didn't seem particularly interested."

Paige bit back a laugh. "Well, in fairness to Costco, there are time constraints to consider. Okay, well, what other ideas did you come up with?"

"Minnie thought, well, maybe she could spice up the inn by, well, maybe offering some *additional* television channels." Mary's eyes widened meaningfully. "You do know what kind of channels I'm talking about?"

Paige chuckled. "Yeah, I understand."

"But that idea is flawed, since I just don't think those channels are, well, novel enough." She made a face to make her point. "Plus, the inn only has eight rooms, so it wouldn't be a significant tourist influx, although we'll take whatever we can get at this point."

"Hmm," Paige said.

"Paige, in truth, we've thought of everything from sand castle contests to tossing a surfboard onto the sand with big teeth marks in it."

Paige gasped. "You were going to let people think a surfer was eaten by a shark?"

Mary nodded her head in measured intervals. "By a great white—we figured that'd bring in news crews and all sorts of Lucy Lookers, but . . ."

"What?"

"Well, somebody really did spot a shark off the public beach, and we didn't want some kid playing daredevil at that point and trolling around on his surfboard."

"I'm with you on that one," Paige said. "Was there anything else you thought about?"

"Well, as you know, Jeanette is really tall, and Minnie is a talented seamstress . . ."

"Yes?" Paige prompted.

"Well, I suggested that Minnie make a big, furry Sasquatch costume, and that we could make a video of Jeanette on the beach—you know, with her sort of taking big strides across the sand and with her head turned, facing the camera. I mean, surely that would create a stir."

Paige bit back a chuckle. "And how did Jeanette feel about this idea?"

"She didn't talk to me for two weeks, but in my defense, the woman does wear a size thirteen shoe." Mary sighed dejectedly. "Paige, we have to try our plan."

"But Gram, even if we do manage to litter the beach with agates, how are you going to get the word out?"

"That's easy. Jeanette still writes the occasional features article for the local newspaper. I know our paper is small, but she has a friend with the AP service. She's sure she can get the article picked up. Even if it only runs in the Portland paper to start, we're good to go."

"You think so?"

"Oh, sure. Jeanette has a six-year-old grandson—cute as a bug's ear, with red hair, freckles, and missing his two front teeth. She plans to take a digital shot of him holding a handful of agates and beaming at the camera. Really, you have to meet this kid. Nobody could resist him."

"Nobody?"

"I'm telling you, the kid is the spitting image of Ron Howard when he played the part of Opie Taylor on *The Andy Griffith Show*."

"That kid *was* cute," Paige admitted.

Mary nodded. "Wyatt has a strawberry blond cast to his hair when the light hits it just right. Did you happen to notice?"

"We're not talking about Wyatt," Paige said pointedly.

Mary looked searchingly into Paige's eyes. "Will you please help us? If I wasn't injured, I would do it myself. But I don't know what else to do. I've lived here all my life, Paige. I can't bear to see the town die—and she won't—as long as we can keep the tourists coming until the roads are fixed."

"The town's a 'she'?"

"Well, of course *she* is."

"Well, in that case, of course I'll help you. When do we start?"

"Tomorrow night."

Chapter Five

Paige woke early the next morning to the sound of crashing waves—the very waves that had lulled her to sleep the evening before. To her surprise, she woke feeling refreshed. She had gone to bed exhausted, and after having heard her grandmother's news the evening before, she had expected she would toss and turn all night. But there was just something about the ocean air.

Paige padded softly from her bedroom to the bathroom to freshen up. She decided to take a quick shower and scrubbed her hair clean with the shampoo she found beside the tub. Once done, she combed out her hair and then dressed quickly in jeans and a white cable-knit sweater. Moments later, she found Mary up and dressed in the kitchen, pouring two cups of coffee.

"Let me get that!" Paige said, scurrying to her grandmother's side. "You sit down and rest that foot."

"People keep telling me that. I wonder, how do you really 'rest' a foot?"

"You know very well how," Paige scolded.

Mary chuckled. "Hey, I didn't ask, but how's your dad?"

"He's great. Business is good, he's healthy and happy, and all is well."

"And you—any young man in your life?"

Paige, who had just taken a steaming hot sip of coffee, nearly sprayed it out of her mouth. Her grandmother was never one to hedge when she wanted answers to questions. "Uh, no, there's no man in my life right now. My job keeps me so busy."

Mary sat back in her chair, holding the coffee mug poised in front of her face and watching Paige speculatively. "Wyatt sure grew into a fine-looking man. Don't you agree? Of course, he was always handsome."

"Don't even go there, Gram," Paige warned. "I didn't come here looking for romance. I came here to see you."

"Yes, but why not kill two birds with one stone?"

"And what makes you think I'm interested in romance? What makes you think Wyatt is interested in romance?"

"That boy loved you with everything in him," Mary commented, smiling wistfully. "I think every woman on this earth longs for that kind of love . . ."

"We were kids!" Paige scoffed. "Neither of us knew what we wanted. We were too young to know what love is."

"If you say so," Mary said.

The two sat quietly for long moments, lost to their respective thoughts. "I'm sorry," Mary said finally. "I didn't mean to upset you. It's a funny thing."

"What is?" Paige asked softly.

"Well, your mother fell in love when she was just a teenager—with the wrong man and for all the wrong reasons. They were both too young . . ."

"And it was all wrong," Paige cut in adamantly, "every bit of it." She shook her head and watched her grandmother gravely. "Nothing good came of it—nothing."

Her grandmother shook her head vigorously, her eyes wide

with alarm. She reached across the table and took Paige's hand. "Paige, something good came from it, something wonderful," Mary said softly, her mouth now curved in a serene smile.

Paige watched her questioningly. "What, Gram—what good came from my mother's selfish choices?"

"You did!" Mary said, giving Paige's hand a final pat. "And later, Don did too."

Paige smiled softly. She couldn't argue with that.

"But you and Wyatt . . . ," Mary mused.

"What about me and Wyatt?"

Mary sighed. "Normally, I would never encourage two youngsters to start a life together—to get married, but you two . . . you're both old souls, kindred spirits. You were a matched set. You probably still are."

As if on cue, Wyatt sauntered into the kitchen, whistling a happy tune. He stopped short of the table, sensing some tension in the room. "Morning all," he said tentatively.

"Good morning," Mary said too brightly. "Coffee?"

"Do you have to ask?" he said, furrowing his brows as he glanced between granddaughter and grandmother. He poured coffee into a travel mug, added a couple scoops of sugar, and then sat down at the table. "What, no eggs and bacon?" he asked Mary.

She chuckled and glanced at Paige. "He's so funny." She turned back to him. "If *you're* making eggs and bacon, I'll take my eggs sunny side up and the bacon extra crisp. Paige, have you got any requests?"

Wyatt grinned. "Ah, if only I had the time to cook breakfast for you two lovely ladies, but unfortunately, duty calls."

He rose from the table, gave them another speculative glance, and then strode from the room. He returned half a minute later. "Oh, and there's one more thing." He wagged a warning finger at Mary. "I'm going to figure out what you're up to. Mark my words, young lady, I'm on to you."

He turned to Paige. "Are you free for dinner?"

Paige glanced at Mary, who nodded. "Of course she's free for dinner."

Once she heard the door close behind Wyatt, Paige turned toward her grandmother. "I can't go to dinner with him. If tonight marks the start of your plan, don't I need to be here?"

Mary shook her head. "Jeanette's got it covered. She took a bag of agates with her last night. Of course, we'll want to get several bagged up, in preparation for our clandestine adventures, but we have time. Maybe after Wyatt takes you to dinner, you can suggest a walk on the public beach, to get your bearings."

Paige laughed nervously. "I don't know about all this, Gram."

"I know you don't. You just have to trust me."

Paige's eyes suddenly widened. "It just occurred to me . . ."

"What's that?"

"You'll need me to stay here all summer long."

"Is that a problem?"

"Gram, I have a job, a life . . ."

Mary met her gaze. "I know. Honey, if you could stay just as long as you can manage, I'm sure I can take over soon. I'll be back on this foot in no time."

"How long did the doctor say you'll need to be off of it?"

"Oh, it won't be for long."

"Gram," she said sternly.

Mary shook her head. "Oh, I don't know. If I don't need surgery, then it'll be eight weeks or so. If it turns out I need surgery . . . who knows?"

"You might need surgery?" Paige cried in a shrill voice. "Why didn't you tell me the injury is serious? You *will* use those crutches, understood?"

Mary made a mock-frightened face. "Yes, ma'am."

"Gram, I'm not kidding. You will stay off that foot if I have to stay here all summer to see that you do."

"Whatever you say is fine, dear."

Paige suddenly wondered, had she just been bamboozled?

Paige spent the better part of her second day on the Oregon coast policing her grandmother's every move. Keeping Mary down was akin to keeping a toddler's hands out of a cookie jar—virtually impossible.

By day's end, Paige was exhausted, and she was splayed out on the couch when Wyatt walked into the family room. He immediately noticed the fatigue on her face.

"She'll wear you out," he said succinctly. "*I* can't keep up with her."

"You're not kidding!" Paige noticed Wyatt was still in uniform. "Are you off work yet?"

He nodded.

"How was your day?" she asked, as she sat up.

"Probably easier than yours. Hey, what's in the pile of boxes over there? Anything you need me to carry someplace for you? If so, I'm at your disposal."

Paige glanced with alarm at the obtrusive pile of boxes in the corner. She really should have moved them.

"That's a lot of boxes," Wyatt observed, studying the stack. "What's in them?"

"Oh, uh, I don't know what's in them," Paige said with a distracted wave.

"Let's have a look," Wyatt said cheerfully, and to Paige's horror, he took a step forward to check them out. She rose in the span of a blink and blocked his way.

He watched her questioningly, through narrowed, suspicious eyes. "What's in them, Paige?"

She shrugged. "Nothing for you to worry about, I'm sure. You've had a long day."

Wyatt cocked his head to the side and stroked his jaw. He attempted to take another step forward, but she physically blocked him again. He shot another glance at the boxes. "You don't know what's in them, then?"

"Well, sure, there's some . . . stuff . . . in them."

"Stuff?" he echoed. He watched her curiously, a smile pulling at the corners of his mouth. By now, she had him by the biceps and was forcibly pushing him back.

He grinned down at her face. "If I didn't know better, I'd think you didn't want me to know what's in those boxes. But really, Paige, I can carry them anywhere you need them to go. Does Mary want them stored in the garage?"

"I . . . don't know. But if she does, I'll do it. They, uh, aren't heavy, and uh, Gram said something about me going through them to find out what's inside . . ."

"If you haven't looked inside, how do you know they're not heavy?" he asked. "And where did you say they came from?"

"I didn't say," she muttered, and then roused herself when he laughed. "Oh, well, Gram was cleaning out her attic . . ."

"With a broken foot?" he said, angling a suspicious look her way. "I don't think so. And I know I would remember seeing those boxes."

"No, I mean, she brought them down from the attic *before* she broke the foot . . . and . . . the boxes were covered by a blanket, so you probably didn't notice them before."

"You are a terrible liar," he said with an affectionate smile, as if he found her inability to be deceptive, cute.

"I'm not . . . lying. I mean"—she averted her eyes—"why would I lie? What reason would I have to lie? I mean, really, why? Why, Wy—I mean, Wyatt?" she finished with a sigh.

"See there! I know you're lying. I'm a trained law enforcement officer, and I know when someone's lying. It's all about the body language. You can't even look at me," he said in measured tones. "Plus, you're rambling on like a locomotive without brakes. See, there," he repeated, wagging a finger in her face, "you can't even look at me."

She tugged her eyes to his. "I can too."

"So let me see inside the boxes."

"They're private."

"Private boxes?"

"Yes. Private boxes."

"If you say so," he finally relented. "Are you still up for dinner?"

"I am if you are. Are you?"

"Absolutely—I'll go change and I'll be back in thirty minutes."

"Can you give me forty-five?"

"Okay, sure," he said. He turned and strode across the room, but paused to glance at the boxes. "These are private boxes—right."

When Paige heard the door close behind him, she spun around in a frantic circle, unsure what to do. Mary suddenly appeared in the room.

"Gram, we have to hide the boxes!" Paige cried.

"I heard. Honey, there's a hand truck in the mudroom. Do you think you can manage to load up the boxes?"

"Where do I put them?"

"Uh, your room, for now."

"Will do."

Paige hurried to retrieve the hand truck and rolled it into the family room. She lifted the first box, surprised by its weight, and surprised she would be surprised by its weight. It was a box of rocks, after all.

She stacked them three high and made four trips into her room. By the time she finished, she was out of breath and hadn't even begun readying for dinner.

She hurriedly dressed in a skirt and blouse, and then dashed into the bathroom to freshen up. Studying herself in the mirror, she noticed a guilty look in her eye and a bead of perspiration on her brow. Wow—she realized she'd make a lousy spy, and desperately hoped Wyatt wouldn't grill her about those boxes anymore.

Suddenly, she heard his deep voice coming from the family room. He had just left. Why was he back so soon?

"Well, hey there, Mary," she heard him say. "What happened to those 'private' boxes?"

"What boxes?" Mary said innocently, and Paige winced.

Paige heard Wyatt's deep, throaty chuckle. "You know, the boxes stacked in the corner over there about fifteen minutes ago."

"You said you'd be back in forty-five minutes," Mary said.

"Aha!" Wyatt shouted. "Caught you! So you admit there were boxes in that corner. And obviously you heard Paige's and my conversation before. My guess is you were listening in the whole time."

"What boxes?" Mary said, and then shook her head. "I mean, what the heck did you just say, Wyatt?"

"What boxes, indeed?" he said, stroking his chin thoughtfully.

When Paige stepped into the living room, feeling anything but refreshed and ready for an evening out, Wyatt searched her face. "What happened to the boxes, Paige?"

"What boxes?" she said, glancing at Mary and shrugging her thin shoulders. Mary shrugged in return.

Wyatt folded his arms across his chest. "You know very well which boxes—both of you."

"Oh, oh!" Paige said. "You mean the boxes that were in the family room, when you were . . . here . . . before."

"Yeah, I mean those boxes."

"I moved them."

"I could have helped you."

She shook her head. "I didn't need any help. You're early."

"Yes, yes I am. Is that a problem?"

"Well, no, but generally, when a woman asks for forty-five

minutes to get ready for a dinner date, and the man shows up fifteen minutes later, the man can count himself fortunate that the woman is ready."

"Well, I'm counting it a minor miracle that you're ready in fifteen minutes *and* had the time to move those boxes. They looked heavy to me. How's your back?" He reached a hand around her and she felt a flutter of awareness as his hands skimmed her blouse.

"Why are you so concerned about those boxes?" Paige asked, attempting to both keep her voice steady and to turn the tables on him.

"Yes, Wyatt, why?" Mary echoed.

"Wyatt," Paige said reasonably, "do you always get so worked up about other people's private boxes?"

He opened his mouth to speak, but then clamped it shut. Finally, he said, "I know what you're trying to do here. You're deflecting. Good technique, by the way."

"I'm really hungry," Paige said. "Are you? I imagine you are, after having worked all day."

"I'm hungry," he conceded, his eyes still narrowed and suspicious.

"What—nobody throw any donuts at you today?" Mary asked, biting back a chuckle.

"No!"

"Well, let's get a move on then," Paige said cheerfully. "I don't know about you, but I have a hankerin' for some seafood." Paige kissed her grandmother on the cheek and strode toward the front door. She paused. "Are you coming, Wyatt?"

"Yeah, I'm coming," he mumbled. "And I'll tell you what *I* have a hankerin' for. I want the truth, and nothing but the truth."

Chapter Six

Wyatt was still scowling as he and Paige entered the seafood restaurant. It was probably the nicest of Agate Cove's three restaurants. Paige feared it was doomed to be a business fatality should Agate Cove's tourist industry combust over the summer.

Seated across from each other in a booth overlooking the ocean, the couple watched each other thoughtfully for a couple of moments. Finally, Wyatt spoke. "What are you and Mary up to?"

Paige sighed. "Wyatt, I don't know why you're so bent on believing Gram and I are up to something."

He raised a pointer finger and aimed it her way. "Look, yesterday I told you Mary was up to something, and after meeting her and her friends for dinner, you were on board, and now I have to think you're on board with whatever *they're* up to."

"That's ridiculous. Let's stop worrying about Gram. If I promise to keep an eye on her, will you stop worrying? I don't know why you're so worked up anyway."

"If you must know, I . . . care about her. She's been good to me. She's letting me live in her apartment and won't take any rent money. Heck, half the time she feeds me, and she makes great coffee. I'm . . . a bit protective of her. She's like a grandmother to me."

Paige reached a hand across the table and squeezed his arm. "That's sweet, Wyatt. I know she's fond of you too."

"Okay, so what's she up to?"

"Arrgghh," Paige groaned. "Nothing! Can we have a nice dinner together, since, well, up until yesterday, we hadn't seen each other for a very long time?"

Wyatt grew silent and reached across the table to take her hand. His sincere eyes bored into hers. "You know, it's been ten years since you and I last saw each other—since we really last spoke . . ."

"What is it?" Paige prompted softly.

"It's as if we parted yesterday—as if time had stood still."

Paige understood what he meant. Shouldn't she feel awkward sitting across the table from the man she had essentially jilted ten years before? Instead, it felt comfortable, familiar—and the reality of that discovery perplexed her.

Yesterday, she had sensed hurt on Wyatt's part—a pain *she* had caused him—but today, only a matter of hours later, it was as if her transgressions had been forgiven. Perhaps Wyatt understood that she had made the best choice for both of them all those years ago. Regardless, she wouldn't ask him how they could remain amiable in light of the past. Maybe someday, before she went home to San Diego, she would ask him. But for tonight, she would simply enjoy his company.

She was grateful he seemed to forget his suspicions about Mary and her friends—and now her—and the two reminisced about old times over her favorite seafood, Dungeness crab. They steered away from heavy topics like her mother, and the hurt her mother had caused her when she had left her at Agate

Cove, but instead talked about their lives during the intervening years since each had left the Oregon coast.

To Paige's surprise, the time flew by, and soon it was nearing dusk. "Would you like to take a quick walk on the beach?" Wyatt asked, and Paige smiled. She had intended to ask him to take a walk.

Paige suddenly remembered that she was wearing heels, but cast aside any worries. She could easily take off her shoes and walk on the sand barefoot.

Soon the couple arrived at Agate Cove's public beach, which extended the length of the town proper. Wyatt parked in a lot off the sand, and Paige quickly shed her heels. Fortunately, she had brought along a coat, since there was a chill in the air.

Like her, Wyatt shed his dress shoes, and then rolled up the dress slacks he wore. He grabbed a Windbreaker from his truck, and the two headed for the sand.

They walked in silence for a while, Paige glancing off to take in the sights and sounds of the surf. She noticed the beach was empty of beachcombers. "It's sad," she said, and Wyatt instantly understood her meaning.

"It looks like a ghost beach," he said. "And if something doesn't give, Agate Cove will soon be a ghost town."

Paige stopped walking and tipped her face to his. "What can the residents do, Wyatt?"

He reached a hand to her face, to pull back a tendril of hair the wind had hold of, and then smiled sadly. "I don't know. Hope for the best, I guess."

"But isn't there something we can *do?*"

"Short of heroic measures, I don't know."

"But Wyatt, if a citizen or group of citizens tried to do something to assure the survival of the town, you'd view them as heroic, wouldn't you?"

Wyatt gave her a puzzled glance. "Well, yeah, I guess, provided they didn't break any laws."

Paige nodded and continued walking along the beach. Wyatt matched her pace.

"Why, Paige? Do you have something up your sleeve? If so, tell me."

She waved off his suggestion. "Oh, no—but I wish I did. I'd do anything to save this place. It means so much to Gram."

Wyatt reached for her hand and held it as they walked—as he had often done when they were kids. And just like when they were kids, Paige felt his warmth radiate up her arm and through her—as if its ultimate destination was her very heart.

Suddenly, she tugged her hand away and stopped. What was she doing holding Wyatt's hand? They didn't even know one another anymore. Walking along the beach—arguably a romantic setting—she could easily be drawn into something false—well, perhaps real, but only for a fleeting moment. She couldn't start something with Wyatt that she simply couldn't finish. She had a life to return to.

Wyatt stood frozen beside her, his face betraying absolutely no emotion. Finally, he smiled a ghost of a smile and continued walking along the beach.

Paige hurried to catch up with him, but crossed her arms over her chest. Somehow, the gesture felt childish, but it couldn't be helped. It was best for him that when she says goodbye this time, she leaves his heart intact—and her own.

When Wyatt spoke, he seemed to have read her thoughts. But they had always had an ability to finish one another's sentences, to know what the other was thinking. "I'm a big boy now, Paige. You can't hurt me," he said.

She forced her eyes to meet his. "Well, the truth is, Wyatt, I think . . . you . . . could hurt me."

On the drive back to her grandmother's house, Paige was quiet. Discreetly, she turned to study Wyatt's handsome profile. She still saw the teenager that he had been, but conceded that the past ten years had only enhanced his good looks. The boyish smoothness of his face had been replaced by a chiseled ruggedness that was softened only by the long lashes currently shielding his eyes from view.

"Do I pass inspection?" he asked, quirking a smile.

"Always," she said without hesitation, and then wondered what had prompted such ridiculous honesty on her part.

He laughed, but sobered quickly. "I would never intentionally hurt you, Paige. You do know that, right? I never meant to hurt you."

She nodded. "Nor I you—but Wyatt, I don't believe in starting something I can't finish."

When he pulled off the road and into a turnout affording a magnificent view of the ocean, she didn't question him, but instead turned to stare out at the Pacific. Even from her vantage point, it looked cold and harsh—but so beautiful it took her breath away.

"I could stare at it for hours on end, never tiring of it," Wyatt observed.

"I know what you mean."

"I could look at you for hours," he said, reaching to take her hand. He was silent for a moment, staring intently at her face. Finally, he spoke. "Who says if we start something, we can't finish it? Come on, Paige—we're adults. We're full-fledged grownups, so what's your excuse now?"

"Excuse?" she said in a tone more shrill than she would have liked.

He raised a hand as if in surrender. "That came out wrong. Forgive me. What I meant to say is, I think—no, I *know*—those old feelings I had for you are still there, and they're not dormant. Even if I didn't want to feel them, they're there. And I have to admit, I'm surprised by the intensity of them. It's been years . . ." He shook his head in wonderment, his blue eyes glistening.

"I don't know what to say."

"Tell me you have feelings for me. I sense that you do."

She couldn't tell him, but instead watched him with anguished eyes. When he reached a gentle hand toward her and laced his fingers through her hair, urging her toward him, she met his lips in a kiss that caused her heart to beat in symphony with the sound of the ocean.

When he pulled back, he searched her eyes, and then smiled in triumph. He wrapped an arm around her and pulled her close to him. Together, they watched the waves break over the rocks below. And although she felt she should leave his arms, she couldn't muster the strength or the will to do it.

"How was your date?" Mary asked Paige. She was sitting up waiting for both her granddaughter and boarder to arrive home.

"It wasn't a date," Paige said.

Mary grinned. "Oh, yes it was."

Paige dropped onto the couch across from Mary's recliner. "How's the foot?"

"It's just fine. How's the heart?"

Paige didn't speak for several moments. "Gram, I loved him so much."

"Honey, I know you did."

"But I couldn't make the same mistakes as my mother. She married so young, and she broke your heart—and Granddad's—and ultimately, mine. I couldn't make her mistakes. I just . . . couldn't."

Mary awkwardly rose from the recliner and crossed the room to sit beside her granddaughter. She took Paige's hand and patted it. "I know, sweetheart, but you're a grown woman now. And Wyatt's definitely a grown man. I don't know if you've noticed, but the man is a looker."

"Oh, I've noticed," Paige admitted. "I've noticed all right."

"Paige, honey, you always talked a lot about making mistakes—well, you talked about your fear of making mistakes—but we learn from our mistakes. And we can't live in fear."

"Do you think I made a mistake by walking away from Wyatt when I was eighteen?"

"Eighteen is too young," Mary admitted. "I believe that. It's the rare couple that survives the struggles of marriage when they wed so young, but you're twenty-eight now. What's wrong with exploring your feelings for Wyatt this go-round?"

"Well, for starters, I'm going home to San Diego at some point, and I get the definite impression that he intends to stay here."

"He did give up a prestigious job in Washington to return here," Mary conceded, "so yes, it's likely he wants to stay. But . . . who knows? In truth, we don't know if 'here' will continue to exist as we all know and love it. Wyatt might have to make some hard choices about his career if this town dies."

"Ah, Gram, personally, I hate hard choices."

"I do too, honey."

Grandmother and granddaughter sat quietly, lost in their own thoughts. Finally, Paige broke the silence. "Gram, how old were you when you married Granddad?"

Mary smiled softly. "Eighteen."

"You never told me that!" Paige exclaimed.

"Times were different back then," Mary said.

Paige accepted the words at face value. "I wish I could have known my granddad," she said wistfully.

"I wish you could have too. He would have loved you. Well, granddaughter, it's time for bed. The girls are coming first thing in the morning to hear Jeanette's report on 'Agate Drop, Summer Sand One.' That's what we're calling it. 'Agate Drop,

Summer Sand,' followed by whatever day it is in the mission. So tomorrow, it'll be . . ."

"I think I follow, Gram," Paige said, chuckling.

"I'm on pins and needles about it myself," Mary said seriously. "I figure Jeanette will head out around three in the morning, make the drop, or drops, depending on how you look at it, and then head home to bed."

"Doesn't she have to work tomorrow?"

"She won't get much sleep—well, any sleep—but we all have to make sacrifices."

Both women started when the phone rang. Mary reached for the cordless phone on the end table beside the sofa. Paige watched her face, as Mary listened to the person on the other end of the line without uttering a single word. Finally, she said "Okay," and hung up.

"What was that about?" Paige asked.

"Jeanette can't make the drop."

"Why can't she?"

"Ralph was supposed to be gone for the night, since he's a long-haul trucker, but he showed up a half hour ago. He said he wanted to surprise her by coming home early. He surprised her all right. Surprised me too," she grumbled.

"What are you going to do about the drop?" Paige asked, surprised at the ease with which she was using her grandmother's lingo.

Mary shook her head, wincing. "It won't do me any good to call the other girls. Minnie is babysitting her granddaughter tonight, and Dori had to drive the detour, to pick up her college-age grandson at the train station in Portland."

"Maybe Dori's grandson can help us out," Paige suggested eagerly.

Mary shook her head curtly. "No, the kid's a dud."

"I'm not even going to ask why you've formed that opinion of the kid."

"You don't want to know," Mary said with certainty. "But you probably don't want to refer to him as a *dud* if Dori's around."

"I'll do my best." Paige yawned. "I think I'll get ready for bed."

"Honey, uh . . . well, with Jeanette out of commission, and the other girls busy, well, I was wondering . . ."

"I'll set my clock for two-thirty."

"Oh, honey, do you mind too much?"

"Would it matter if I did?" She grinned and saluted her grandmother. "Ask not what your town can do for you, but ask what you can do for your town—er, your grandmother's town."

"Honey, you're doing a lot," Mary assured her, nodding her head up and down. "More than you know."

"Oh, I know it," Paige agreed, wondering how her stepfather would feel about all she would be doing for Agate Cove, at the expense of her job.

Chapter Seven

When Paige woke up at 2:30, she found her grandmother up and hobbling around with a backpack full of colorful, unpolished agates.

"Hey, Gram, did you even go to bed last night . . . tonight . . . this morning . . . whatever? You need your rest, you know."

"Couldn't sleep," Mary said succinctly. "I'm too excited about tonight. It's Agate Drop, Summer Sand One, after all."

"True," Paige replied with a yawn. She left her grandmother briefly to slip into a sweatshirt, sweatpants, and her running shoes, lest she need to run from anything, and then entered the kitchen, where Mary thrust a mug full of coffee at her.

"Are you awake?" her grandmother asked in a forceful tone. "Drink the coffee."

"I'm awake, sir!" Paige took a sip of coffee. "Coffee tastes like mud, sir!"

"Oh, stop that," Mary said with a rueful grin. "This is serious."

"Don't I know it," Paige said with chagrin. "I got to thinking, as I was tossing and turning in anticipation of 'Agate Sand, Summer Drop Whatever,' that I know nothing about the tides in that big bad ocean. What if I'm out there dropping agates, and the tide comes in, and I don't see it, and I'm washed out to sea—where that great big, surfboard-eating great white is waiting for me? No one will ever know what became of me, unless, of course, my parts wash up on shore."

"Oh, Paige!" Mary cried. "You're right. It's far too dangerous." She dropped into a chair and dropped her head into her hands. "Oh, the town is dead, but better the town than you!"

"Gram, I'm kidding—well, sort of. Give me a flashlight, and I'll get through tonight, and tomorrow we'll study the tides."

Mary searched her brain. "I really should know when high tide and low tide is, but it escapes me right now."

"I was never very good at pop quizzes either."

"Are you sure you want to do this, Paige? I don't know if I can let you do this." She moaned miserably. "No, I know I don't want you to go. There could be some axe murderer down on that beach, or even a mountain lion, or a . . . a . . . squid could wash up and before it takes its last breath, it could take a bite out of you."

"Do squids bite?" Paige asked, furrowing her brow. "I honestly can't remember if squids bite or not. I know I saw something about them on the Discovery Channel. Funny I don't remember."

"I don't find that particularly funny," Mary said grumpily.

"I do know *I* like to bite into squid, regardless of whether or not they like to bite into me. I really am a big fan of calamari. Do you like calamari, Gram? Truth is, if I run into a squid on the beach, it probably has more to fear from me than I do from it—well, unless it's one of those giant squids . . ."

"Paige, you've gone off on a tangent," Mary moaned. "Oh, honey, I can't let you go."

"Do we really have a choice at this point, Gram? I mean, you've bought a boatload of agates from the 'Television Shopping Show.' It's not like you need twelve boxes of rocks sitting around here collecting dust. Let me go drop some on the beach, and I'm sure tomorrow will be a brighter day for my trouble."

"You think so?"

"Sure," she said with forced cheer. "Tomorrow the town will discover the reason Agate Cove is called Agate Cove, and we'll have officially started Operation Save Agate Cove."

" 'Operation Save Agate Cove,' " Mary repeated. "I kind of like that. Do you like that name better, Paige? We could call our operation 'Operation Save Agate Cove' instead of Agate Drop, Summer Sand One, because honestly, that is kind of a mouthful."

"Yet another detail we'll work out tomorrow," Paige said. "Now pass me those agates—and a flashlight."

Mary passed her the agates and a tiny flashlight, and Paige strode toward the front door. She paused at the threshold and hefted the heavy agates more securely onto her shoulder. "I'll see you soon," she said bravely. Mary looked skeptical and Paige chuckled. "Gram, have no worries. I'll be fine."

She closed the door behind her and crept softly across the front lawn, turning on her tiny flashlight beam intermittently; she was half-afraid Wyatt might somehow spot it from his apartment window.

When she reached the zigzagging trail down to the public beach, she realized her grandmother's property was ideally located for the venture, but that the trail wasn't the most ideal way down. But it couldn't be helped, and she carefully dropped down the trail, keeping her flashlight on only occasionally. When she finally dropped onto the beach below, she heaved a sigh of relief.

She glanced around her, attempting to get her bearings.

Unfortunately, a fog had come in, and she couldn't help rolling her eyes. "Just dandy," she muttered. "I can't see my hand in front of my face."

The seriousness of the situation gripped her. Without a real sense of where she was in relation to the surf, she could very easily be swept out to sea. Additionally, if there were any hazards on the beach, she wouldn't be able to spot them. Should she turn back? She chewed her lip thoughtfully, wondering if she listened intently to the breaking waves, could she gauge her distance from them?

It was worth a try. She could always turn around if she had to. She set out along the sand, but soon discovered that she was walking along dry sand, and it was imperative she drop the agates along the wet sand where the waves broke. But again, she wondered, when was high tide and low tide? What was the best place to drop the agates?

With a frustrated sigh, she decided that she would have to make the best of the situation, and hoped desperately that once she dropped the agates, they wouldn't be swept out to sea by an ultimately receding high tide. Tomorrow she would walk the beach during the light of day in order to select the best placement of the agates.

Tonight she would have to wing it. She reached a hand into the backpack and pulled out a handful of agates. She found she had to move slower than she would have liked, in order to give good agate coverage to any particular location. She practically groaned aloud. A quarter-mile of this—surely her supply of agates wouldn't hold out!

Fearing that she would run out of stones, she began tossing handfuls and simultaneously picked up her pace. She walked briskly, hoping this effort wouldn't prove all for naught the next day.

It was frightening to be walking into a fog without any sense of what might be in front of her face. She searched her memory. Was there a flagpole sunk into the sand anywhere along her path? If so, with her luck, she would probably smack face-first into it.

Of course there wasn't a flagpole sunk into the sand, she told herself. You couldn't sink a flag pole into sand. *What kind of a moron would sink a flagpole into shifting sands? Why, that would be stupid.*

Although there wasn't a flagpole, she did walk smack into a log across her path and tumbled headlong into a wave. She rose up gasping and realized that a large portion of her agates had fallen out of the pack. She didn't bother picking them up, but backed away from the pounding waves.

What the heck am I doing out here? she wondered, as she hurried along the beach, resisting the temptation to turn on her flashlight. It was so dark that the tiny beam of light wouldn't have illuminated more than a foot in front of her, anyway. She shoved her hand into the pack, tossed the agates, and did it again, over and over, until she had emptied the pack.

Attempting to gauge how far she had walked, she finally risked turning on the flashlight and extended her arm out. To her surprise, she spied the dune only yards away from her. The fact that she could see it at all was indicative of a thinning fog. That was good news, except that the fog did afford protection from probing eyes.

What if someone spotted her? How could she explain her walk on the beach? Visitors were not allowed on the beach after dusk per town rules.

She turned back toward her grandmother's, glad she had covered more ground than she had thought. Tomorrow she would obtain a step counter and pace out the beach, for those times like tonight when she couldn't see her hand in front of her face and needed to gauge how far she had walked.

As the fog swirled around her, thinning as she walked, she

felt relief that she could see several yards in front of her now. This time, she managed to avoid a log that was lodged in the sand directly in her path.

She wondered how long she had been gone. It seemed like an eternity and only moments, all at the same time. She hurried toward her grandmother's house. She found herself eagerly anticipating morning, and wondered if the agates would remain on the beach or be swept out to sea. She willed the little agates to stay put.

A thought occurred to her: she should have pressed them down, ever so lightly, with her feet so that they would remain lodged in the wet sand. Surely that might help to assure that they remained on the beach when morning came. Perhaps if she walked close to the surf again, she could manage to walk over many of the agates and lodge them for safekeeping. She kept her eyes peeled for the agates, carefully pressing them into the sand with her feet as she walked along.

Paige finally reached the trail that led back to her grandmother's house. She climbed it slowly, afraid she might slip. A tumble down the steep incline could easily result in injury or death. She turned on the flashlight so she wouldn't make a misstep, and with relief, finally stepped onto her grandmother's manicured lawn.

She started across the lawn, the muscles in her legs protesting the exertion of her walk and climb, but she halted when someone called out her name. That someone was Wyatt.

"Paige, what are you doing out there?" He jogged toward her, a concerned expression on his face.

She froze, glanced down at the empty backpack in her hand, and carefully tossed it behind her. She prayed it landed behind a bush, and that the shrub would obscure it from sight until she could retrieve it later.

She walked toward Wyatt, who met her midway across the lawn. She desperately hoped he wouldn't notice that her clothes were damp. He held a large, police-issue flashlight in his hand and aimed it at her face.

She raised a hand to shield her eyes and he immediately dropped the beam. "I'm sorry," he said. "I was so surprised to see you out here. It's still dark, Paige. What are you doing out here at this time of the morning?"

"What time is it?" she asked.

"It's almost five."

Her eyes widened in surprise. Had she really been gone that long?

Wyatt watched her intently. "Paige, what were you doing out on the public beach at this time of the morning? It's not even open to visitors yet. Did you go down there by yourself? It's not safe out there in the dark."

"Oh, no, no, I didn't go down to the public beach. I was sitting on the crest of the hill, looking out at the beach." She hated lying to him, but what could she do?

"It's too foggy to see anything," he pointed out.

"Oh, I know," she said quickly. "I love listening to the crashing waves. It's so soothing, don't you think?"

"Uh-huh," he muttered doubtfully. "Do you always get up this early?"

"No, I, uh, couldn't sleep. Sometimes . . . I suffer from a little insomnia."

"A little insomnia, as opposed to a lot of insomnia?" he asked, watching her suspiciously.

"I couldn't sleep, so I went for a walk. Who knew it was a Federal offense, Wyatt?"

"Don't turn the tables on me, Paige. It's dark, foggy, and if you'll remember, there's a cliff not so far in that direction." He pointed westward, toward the end of the property.

"Which I am well aware of," she said.

"Okay, look . . ." He glanced at his watch. "I have to go to work. You should get inside. It's just not safe out here."

"I have my flashlight." She held it up for him to see.

"You call that a flashlight!" He shook his head. "Come on. You need to get inside."

At the front door of her grandmother's house, Wyatt paused to search her face. "Paige, promise me you won't go outside unless it's during the light of day. You don't know this country like your grandmother does, or me. One misstep and you really could tumble into the water. And none of us would be the wiser."

His concern was heartfelt, and so sincere, but she couldn't make that promise. She attempted to distract him instead. "Have you had breakfast? I'd be happy to make you bacon and eggs."

He emitted a long sigh. "No, but . . . no thanks. I have to get moving. Stay in the house, okay?"

"Sure," she said agreeably, and then turned and walked into the house. She closed the door behind her and stood with her back pressed against the wood. She took a deep breath to slow her pounding heart.

Suddenly, her grandmother flew into the foyer, her crutches moving like chopsticks on the tile. "Oh, Paige, I was so worried."

"Wyatt saw me," she said breathlessly.

"What? No!"

"It was so dark, he didn't realize I was wet, so he didn't put two and two together and figure out that I really was on the beach."

Mary's hands rose to her face. "Oh, Paige, did you fall into the ocean?"

"No, no, I just slipped in the wet sand—no big deal." Paige just couldn't bring herself to tell Mary she'd fallen headlong into a wave. It would give her grandmother too many sleepless nights.

"What did you tell Wyatt?"

"I told him I couldn't sleep and that I was sitting outside listening to the ocean."

"Did he believe you?"

Paige shrugged. "Hard to tell. It was apparent, however, that he thinks I'm insane for walking around the yard when there's a decidedly dangerous drop-off at the end."

Mary mulled over her words. "Okay, so he doesn't know you were on the public beach. That's good, anyway." She sighed. "Let's sit down and talk about the mission."

"Oh, Gram," Paige moaned. "Can we wait and talk when the girls show up? I think I need a few hours' sleep or I won't be any good to anyone."

"Sure, sure, honey—of course—you need sleep."

Paige kissed Mary on the cheek and headed to her room. She tugged off her shoes and slipped out of the jacket and sweatshirt, exposing a tank top beneath. She took off her sweatpants, and fell onto the bed with a fatigued sigh.

Only morning would tell if there was a payoff to her night-time adventure.

"Paige, rise and shine—the girls are here!"

"What time is it?"

"It's already noon."

Paige sat up, attempting to shrug off sleep's hold. She rubbed her eyes. "Noon?"

"Yes, I called the girls and asked them to wait until noon to come since you needed sleep."

"What about their customers?"

"What customers?" Mary said sadly.

"I need a shower," Paige said and moved like a sleepwalker toward the shower and pulled on the faucet. She gave the water a moment to warm up, and then undressed and stepped under the spray. It felt glorious against her skin, and she was hard-pressed to leave the warmth of it. But duty called.

She hurriedly combed out her hair and dressed in jeans and a T-shirt. A quick look in the mirror confirmed that she looked tired, with dark circles framing her lower lids. Who knew her beach adventure would wear her out so much? But she suspected it was less the actual endeavor that wore her out and more the anticipation of it, and then running into Wyatt in the front yard. It had been a shock. More shocking was finding him at her grandmother's kitchen table now, and as a result, privy to her late rising.

"Are you just getting up?" he asked, his brows knitted in concern.

She attempted a sunny smile. "Uh, well, yeah, I am, sort of."

"Would you like some breakfast—er, lunch?" Mary asked. "Wyatt brought fish and chips."

"That sounds great," Paige said, smiling at Wyatt. "That was thoughtful of you."

"I'm a thoughtful guy." He eased back in his chair, shifting his nightstick away from his muscular thigh in order to get comfortable. He appeared to be settling in for a long visit.

"Are you staying?" Mary asked him sweetly.

"I thought I might," he said, equally sweetly.

Paige pulled several plates from a kitchen cabinet. Standing behind Wyatt, she glanced pointedly at the back of his head, and then up to meet Mary's eyes.

Mary winced and apparently Wyatt noticed. "Something on your mind, Mary?" he said smoothly.

"No, nothing," she said too quickly, and sat down as Paige set the plates on the table.

"Oh, we've eaten," Dori said, and passed Paige back the empty plates. "Minnie, Jeanette, and I ate at the diner earlier."

"Oh, okay," Paige said, and returned three plates to the cabinet. She began serving up the fish and chips to Wyatt, her grandmother, and herself. She sat down at the table, in the only open chair—beside Wyatt. It was a tight fit, and she felt self-conscious as the four older women smiled her way.

Mary's three friends sat quietly while the others ate their lunch. Wyatt commented, "Wow, I don't think I've ever seen you ladies so subdued. Is there something wrong? As your local law enforcement officer, I am here to protect and to serve. Is there anything I can do to protect or to serve you?"

Jeanette arched her brows flirtatiously and Wyatt raised a hand. "Okay, I walked right into that one," he said quickly. "But no more innuendos, please—you're embarrassing me."

Jeanette opened her mouth to speak, and Wyatt shot her a warning glance. "You think you're going to make me so uncomfortable that I'm going to leave. It won't work this time," Wyatt warned.

"Does it usually work?" Paige asked with interest.

"Yeah, but since you've been here, they're mighty tame. If you weren't here, it'd be their express mission to see my face turn bright red."

"You're a blond. You turn red easily," Dori commented.

"Well, it's not going to work today," he said, tilting his head to the side and stroking his chin thoughtfully. "You all are up to something, and I'm going to find out what it is."

Suddenly, Wyatt's police radio crackled to life. He snapped it off his belt and listened to the dispatcher on the other end. She spoke in ten-codes, the language of cops, and the women at the table couldn't understand a word of it. When Wyatt replaced the radio on his belt, he grimaced.

"Do you have to leave?" Mary asked in a saccharin tone.

"Yeah," he said in a frustrated voice. He rose from the table, shaking his head. He didn't bother saying good-bye, but instead wagged a warning finger at the group and then strode out of the room.

"Bye, dollface!" Jeannette called after him.

Chapter Eight

I didn't think he'd ever leave," Mary said. "Okay, girls, let's talk."

Paige found herself pelted with questions about her early-morning adventure. She raised a hand to silence the group. "One question at a time, please," she said, chuckling.

"How long did it take you to distribute the agates?" Jeanette asked.

"About . . . two hours," she said. "It was so foggy, I couldn't see my hand in front of my face. And since it was so dark, I couldn't see the surf. I kept expecting a big wave to come in and sweep me out to sea."

"What'd you do?" Dori asked fearfully.

"Well, once I staved off my panic, I realized I could discern where to walk by listening to the waves."

Mary spoke up in a serious tone. "I have to admit, I was a nervous wreck about Paige being out there. We were so eager about our plan, we didn't really take into consideration the danger involved."

The women nodded in agreement.

"I got to thinking last night about all the perils out there," Dori said. "It's true a sneaker wave could come along, or some weirdo could be sleeping on the sand." She shook her head. "I'm not sure this is such a good idea."

"We could go in teams," Minnie suggested.

Mary shook her head. "Girls, we'll need to drop those rocks every morning until summer's end. It makes more sense to go alone, so we'll—you'll—have time to rest between your assignments."

The group pondered Mary's words, and then conceded she was right. They had over ninety days of agate-dropping duty ahead.

"Okay, I've been thinking," Paige spoke up. "I think we four," she aimed a glance at the ladies, excluding her grandmother, "should meet at the public beach later today. I think it's important we walk the beach, each counting the steps it takes us to walk from one end to the other."

"We should each get a step counter," Jeanette suggested, "for accuracy."

"I was thinking that too," Paige said. "Anyway, if we all have an idea of how many steps it will take us to walk from one end of the beach to the other, we'll have a better sense of security when we're out there on those foggy, dark nights—I mean, early mornings. Hey," she said suddenly, "any word on the agates I dropped last night? I was so afraid they'd be washed out to sea."

Jeanette smiled broadly. "Success!" she cried eagerly. "Since it's Saturday, and my grandson doesn't have school, I planted a little bug in his ear—told him to ask his mom to take him down to the beach. The little guy's awfully persuasive, and they went. And . . . lo and behold, he found handfuls of agates. He came into the diner later just beaming."

"That's awesome!" Paige cried. "I really didn't think it would work. I was so afraid the waves would carry the agates out to sea. We'll want to get down there and take note of where I dropped them. Maybe I managed to hit on the right spot in relation to the waves."

"You did!" Dori said eagerly. "I took an early-morning walk myself, just to check it out. Paige, you did a great job of distributing the rocks in a natural pattern."

Suddenly, Paige's eyes widened. "Could you see my footprints in the sand?"

Dori furrowed her brow. "You know what? Not that I noticed—but besides, it wouldn't really matter. Anybody could have left footprints behind."

"True," she said, visibly relaxing.

"Okay, okay, this is wonderful," Mary said, "but I worry . . ."

"What?" Jeanette prompted.

"I am concerned about safety." Mary sighed. "In the future, when any one of you goes down there, safety must be paramount. Never, ever, turn your back on the ocean. Carry a flashlight that affords a powerful beam, even if you only turn it on occasionally, and"—she awkwardly rose from the table and retrieved several items from a nearby drawer—"each of you will always carry these." She dumped a pile on the table. Paige was first to reach for one of the items.

"Is this a stun gun?" she asked incredulously. "And what's this other thing?" She read the label. "Pepper spray?—Gram, where did you get this stuff?"

"Yes, that's a stun gun," Mary said. "And that's pepper spray. I got them at the police supply shop in Portland. And you'll each be sure to carry them with you. We don't want any fatalities down there."

"You would have made a great cop, Mary," Jeanette observed.

The others echoed their agreement.

"I always thought so," Mary said seriously.

Later, Paige stood on the public beach, along with Dori, Jeanette, and Minnie. The wind whipped their hair and Paige wished the cold wasn't so biting. It was late May, for Pete's sake.

"Okay," Paige called above the wind, "let's head over to the dune. We'll walk from there to the other end of the beach."

The ladies nodded and then braced against the biting wind to cross to the dune. Once there, Paige took charge again. "Okay, pull out your step counters and let's get moving."

As they walked, the women chatted among themselves. Onlookers would have wondered at the synchronization of their walk—unintended, but happening just the same. They looked like four soldiers about to embark upon a mission—and in fact, they were.

The group stayed close to the incoming waves, taking note of the placement of the agates. Paige couldn't help beaming when she spied the rocks lying parallel to the breaking waves, just waiting for beachcombers to come along and scoop them up.

"I suppose I should pick up a brochure about the tides," she observed to her friends.

"I have some in my souvenir shop," Dori said loudly, over the sound of the wind and waves.

"I do think you've done a good job out here, Paige," Jeanette commented. "You really did manage to achieve a natural agate distribution pattern."

"I think so too," Minnie said.

"We should also take note of any obstacles in our path," Paige said, scanning the beach. Her eyes lit on the log she'd likely tripped over before. She aimed a finger at it. "You know, we're going to have to be really careful about logs. They come in all the time. If one was picked up by a wave and then came sailing back in, someone could get hurt."

"That's true," Jeanette agreed. "Let's just hope we have some visibility when we're out here."

"There'll be plenty of early mornings we don't," Paige pointed out. "Truly, I couldn't see my hand in front of my face this morning. It was scary."

Paige felt Dori shudder beside her. "I don't know if I can do this," she said, a hysterical edge to her voice.

The women stopped walking. "Dori, you have to," Minnie said. "Think about the town—about your shop. It's the only way."

"But . . . I mean, can't we bring other people in on our plan? Why should we take all the risk and responsibility?"

"No," Jeanette said firmly, "the fewer people who know about this, the better."

The group had reached the end of their walk and were standing at the base of the sandy hill that led upward to Paige's grandmother's property.

"It's really not such a long walk," Minnie observed cheerfully. "We can do this, girls! Heck, Paige has already done it once. We can sure do our parts. Can't we?" she urged, sounding much like the cheerleader she had been during her high school years.

Suddenly, she thrust her hand out and nodded at her friends. Each one laid her hand on top of the others' hands until all hands were on the pile.

To her own surprise, Paige called out, "Operation Save Agate Cove!"

"Save Agate Cove!" the women chanted.

"Hey, I like that name better than the other one," Minnie commented. "Operation Save Agate Cove—that has a nice ring to it, and it's easier to remember."

"True," the others echoed.

Finally, the group turned back and started their trek back to the parking lot. Unbeknownst to them, Wyatt sat in his parked patrol car, watching them. His binoculars were trained on their faces, but since he couldn't read lips, he couldn't make out what each was saying.

By the time the women reached the parking lot, he was waiting, leaning nonchalantly against his patrol car. "Ladies!" he called out, tipping his hat to each one of them.

He was gratified when they looked startled to see him, and he laughed outright when Jeanette gave him an angry stare. "I've put people in jail for less than that!" he called, unperturbed, and with a hearty chuckle.

"You won't take me alive, copper!" she taunted. "But come on over here. You can make sure I die happy!"

Once again, Wyatt's face flamed red. It was still red when he sauntered over to Paige's economy car.

"Did you hear what your friend just said to me?" he asked her.

Paige played dumb. "Uh, no—what'd she say?"

"Well, I'm not going to repeat it," he said, aghast. "I'm a gentleman."

"What are you doing here?" she asked him pointedly.

"Watching you ladies," he said, unapologetically.

"Why? Don't you have anything better to do? I'm sure someone is committing a crime somewhere between the North and South holes."

He watched her, nonplussed. "Trying to deflect again, aren't we? Are you ladies, perchance, committing any crimes I should be aware of?"

"No," she said testily, "unless walking on the beach is a crime."

It occurred to her that their efforts to save Agate Cove might be wasted if Wyatt didn't stop his apparent surveillance of them. She wished she could bring him in on their secret, but she couldn't. He was the law, and she would never want to jeopardize his good standing in the community by forcing him to keep their secret. Not that he would.

"I should go," she said crisply.

She turned to leave and he took her arm. "Hey," he said, his eyes boring into hers, "I didn't mean to upset you. Are you all right?"

She attempted to shake off her nervousness, but she felt on edge. "I'm fine, Wyatt—just tired, I guess."

"Is it the insomnia?"

She nodded. "Uh, yeah, it's the insomnia all right."

"Anything you want to talk about? I have to stop by the jail, but you're welcome to follow me. We can talk there."

"Agate Cove has a jail?"

"Yep, it's been around for fifty years, has only two cells, and probably couldn't keep Jeanette secure behind bars." He chuckled at the image of the mouthy woman lodged in the Agate Cove jail. "Anyway, I've taken up residence there, since I need an office." He reached a hand to stroke her windblown cheek. "Wanna follow me?"

She hesitantly met his gaze. Although she suspected she should get home, she agreed to follow him. She climbed into her car and then waited for Wyatt to pull out of the lot before she followed. She questioned the wisdom of going anywhere with him at this point, since she might divulge something she shouldn't—but she couldn't deny she wanted to be with him.

They drove less than a mile, to an old building Paige immediately recognized. It was located behind the convenience store in town, and had definitely seen better days.

"I know this building," Paige said as she climbed out of her car and watched Wyatt stride over to her. "But I never knew what it was." She glanced at the back of the convenience store in front of them. "I imagine the store owners feel an increased sense of security with you back here."

Wyatt shrugged. "I suppose so. Hey, you'll want to keep your coat on inside. The place barely has heat."

Paige leaned into her car to retrieve her coat and slipped into it. Despite the coat's bulk, she felt Wyatt's warm hand on her lower back as he led her into the antiquated jail.

Stepping into the jail was like stepping back in time. Only one semi-large room, the building housed an old desk and two chairs on one end, with two cells against the eastern wall. A bunk was pressed against a corner in each cell. A single door on the north wall led to what Paige surmised was a bathroom.

Wyatt took the chair behind the desk and urged her to sit across from him. She sat down and then hugged her coat around her. "You weren't kidding about the lack of heat," she observed.

Wyatt rose briefly to turn on a space heater and tilted it in her direction. Paige smiled her thanks.

He returned to his chair and then tipped back, watching her, his arms folded behind his head.

She felt uncomfortable under his scrutiny. "Why are you staring at me like that?" she asked.

"You're beautiful," he said simply, "but you're also up to no good."

"And why would you say that?" she demanded haughtily. "Why would you ever presume I would be up to no good? I think I'm actually insulted by that remark, Wyatt."

He only chuckled at her indignation. "Didn't mean to insult you," he said good-naturedly. "So, are you enjoying your visit to the coast?"

"Don't interrogate me, Wyatt!" she snapped, and he burst out laughing.

"I wasn't interrogating you. I was making small talk. Should I be interrogating you?"

"No!"

"Why would I want to interrogate you? I can think of other things we could do with our time." He arched his brows suggestively.

"No, thank you." Afraid to meet his stare, Paige studied her fingernails, currently filthy and embedded with sand.

Wyatt spied her nails. "Aha! A clue!" he said, grinning like a dope at her. "I don't ever remember a time your nails weren't clean."

"You know what, Wyatt," Paige said with mock sympathy, "I think you're a very bored law enforcement officer."

"Yeah, poor me—come on over here and we'll talk about it." He arched his brows again.

"Wyatt," she said shrilly, "you're a cop! The undersheriff of this county, and you're over there smirking at me, suggesting we engage in what the citizens of this town might regard as . . . improper behavior. I should think you'd want to be a better example for the citizenry of this town."

"Hey, I only meant we could kiss. Besides, we're stuck here between the North and South holes, and as such, crime seems to be on the downswing."

"Well, that's good news, isn't it? You almost sound disappointed."

"You're right. It's a good thing," he said. "It is boring, but good news for the town."

Paige sighed as she glanced around. "Well, now that I've seen the jail, I think I'll be on my way."

"Things to do?" he observed wryly. "Anything you'd like to talk about . . . anything *illegal?*"

Paige rose from the chair with a scowl, and then walked toward the door. Wyatt was out of his chair in a flash and reached the door before she could. She reached for the knob, but he held the door closed with a strong hand planted above her head. "Would you like to join me for dinner?" he asked sweetly.

She met his gaze. "I'm sorry, I have plans."

He quirked a smile. "Anything to do with what I observed on the beach earlier?"

Paige stiffened. *What exactly had he observed?* He'd seen nothing, as far as she could tell. She searched her memory. *What was he talking about?*

"Why the gesture of solidarity?" he asked her, searching her face.

She only shrugged, unsure what he meant.

"You know what I'm talking about—when you ladies put your hands together in some sort of cheer."

Paige waved a dismissive hand. "Oh, that—Minnie used to be a cheerleader. She was . . . feeling nostalgic, talking about when she was a teenager in high school, and she and several friends went down to the beach . . ."

Wyatt waved a dismissive hand this time, effectively cutting her off. He leaned in close to her. "You are a terrible liar. A life of crime would never suit you. I'm telling you, Paige, you may as well fess up to whatever you and your friends are up to. Come on, talk."

"Oh, so if we were up to something—which we're not—you'd expect me to rat out my friends."

"So you admit you're up to something, you and your co-horts. You can tell them that just because they're grandmothers, I'm not going to go easy on them. Tell them if they come forward now, I might be willing to cut a deal."

"Oh, Wyatt," she said with a beleaguered sigh, "I think you need a hobby."

He only laughed, and she hesitantly raised her face to his. He was so close, she could see the flecks of darker blue in his ocean blue eyes. She attempted to take a step back, but her progress was halted by the hard door. Wyatt chuckled and moved even closer to her, pausing long enough to search her eyes. And then he kissed her. And as she always had in the past, she responded to his kiss.

Chapter Nine

Paige climbed into her car and started the engine. She glanced up in surprise when Wyatt ran out of the jail and to his patrol car and got in. Suddenly, the emergency light bar atop his car lit up. Wyatt brought the car around in a flash, paused briefly to roll down his window, and met her eyes. "We may have a fatality at the South Hole."

Paige gasped. "Oh no, how awful!"

"Drive safe," he told her.

"Wy, be careful," she said, and then watched as he pulled away, activating his sirens as the tires of his patrol car hit Highway 101.

Paige drove slowly toward her grandmother's house. She uttered a prayer for whoever might be injured or worse at the collapsed roadway. Currently, a dark fog hovered over the wet road, and she suspected the conditions weren't ideal for someone unfamiliar with the driving conditions.

Safely back at her grandmother's home, she found Mary in her recliner, dozing. When Paige draped a throw blanket over her, she started awake.

"I'm sorry I woke you."

"No, no, I'm glad you did. How'd it go down on the public beach? Did you and the girls get a chance to count out your steps?"

Paige nodded. "We did. Of course, when we were done, we found Wyatt waiting for us beside his patrol car. He is so suspicious, Gram."

"He's a cop. It's his nature."

"Gram, I'm not sure we're going to get away with our plan."

"I know you're worried, honey. I am too. But we have to try."

"Oh, Gram, I guess someone might have been killed at the South Hole today."

Mary gasped. "Oh, no!"

"I know. Wyatt went to the call just a while ago."

"Do you know any details?" Mary asked.

Paige shook her head.

"Oh, Lord," Mary said sadly, "that darn road."

"I wonder if the road crew managed to get additional signs up to alert drivers to the road closure and detour?" Paige asked.

"I think they did," Mary said. "I think Minnie mentioned it to me."

"Who's going out tonight to make the drop?" Paige asked with a sigh.

"That's what I needed to talk to you about, honey."

"What is it?" Paige asked, bracing for her answer.

"It's supposed to be Dori's turn, but she chickened out. Minnie said she'd take her turn if she could, except she can't get away tonight, and Jeanette's husband won't be back to work for a day or two . . ."

"I think I'll go take a nap," Paige said resignedly, but paused at the threshold of the family room entrance. "Gram, do you think the ladies really intend to do their parts? If they don't, I just don't know how this plan is going to work."

Mary considered the question. "I do, honey. We're just getting off to a slow start."

Paige nodded and then headed to her bedroom.

"Oh, Paige," Mary called, "your dad called earlier."

Her dad—she had promised to call him often, since it was likely he had work-related questions regarding the Lawton account. "Okay, Gram, I'll call him back now."

Quickly, she dialed her father on her cell phone, and then settled on her bed to talk. The call went to voice mail, and Paige stared at the phone with concern. She shrugged off the worry. Her stepfather was still at work and likely in a meeting.

She laid the cell phone on the stand beside her bed and eased herself against the plump pillow. Suddenly, the phone rang, and Paige answered.

"Hey, honey, when are you coming home?" Don asked.

"Uh, Dad, I may be here a while," she told him.

"Hon, we really miss you around here, but I understand your grandmother needs you there. I have to get back to a meeting, but will you call me soon and let me know how things are going?"

"I will, Dad. I love you."

"I love you too, Paige. Talk to you real soon."

She hung up the phone, and in mere minutes, drifted off to sleep.

She woke hours later to her grandmother shaking her awake. "Honey, it's time."

"Time for what?" Paige moaned.

"Time for Operation Save Agate Cove."

"Oh, yeah," Paige said, as she swung her legs over the bed. She glanced at the clock again. Had she really slept all those hours? She remembered taking a nap, but she must have slept all the way through until now.

She hurried to the bathroom and got ready, and then met her grandmother in the kitchen. "Shoot," she murmured, "I didn't fill a bag with agates to put in the backpack." Her eyes widened in alarm. "Oh, no! I forgot the backpack. When Wyatt caught me this morning, I tossed it behind me into a shrub."

"Honey, relax. It's okay. I found it," Mary said.

"Gram," Paige said sternly, "what were you doing walking around the front lawn?"

"I was using crutches," she assured her.

Mary helped Paige into her coat and passed her the pepper spray and stun gun. Paige eyed the devices suspiciously. "Do you really think I'll need these?"

"We simply cannot take any chances," Mary said firmly.

Paige stuffed the items into her coat and took the backpack from her grandmother. She shifted the pack, adjusting its bulk, and then walked to the front door. Mary remained at her side.

"I hope Wyatt doesn't spot me," Paige said.

"He won't. He isn't home."

Paige's eyes widened.

"It's okay, hon. He called earlier. It turns out he's going to be spending a lot of time in Lincoln City. He said he'll be investigating the fatality accident, so he's likely to be busy for several weeks."

"Do you know when he might come home?"

"Technically, he is home," Mary said. "He'll be staying at his house much of the time he completes the investigation. I understand he'll be doing a lot of back-and-forth driving."

"Poor Wy," Paige commiserated, "having to do that detour."

"I told him you'd call him," Mary commented, "since he asked to talk to you."

"You didn't tell him I was sleeping when he called, did you?" Paige said with a wince.

Mary gave her a baffled look. "Shouldn't I have? I'm sorry."

Paige waved off her concern. "Oh, it's okay, Gram. I just

didn't want Wyatt thinking I sleep all the time. He seemed concerned that I slept in until noon. He's worried about me."

"Well, you had good reason to be sleeping," Mary said protectively, in her defense.

"But he doesn't know that."

"True."

"Okay, I'm going to get a move on," Paige said, and stepped into the early-morning air. To her surprise, the day was clear and the air surprisingly warm. "Hey, what happened to our bad weather?" she asked.

"Maybe spring has finally sprung?" Mary said with a smile. "Now, you be careful out there."

Paige turned and strode to the trail down to the public beach, dropping onto it carefully. She didn't bother turning on the flashlight, since a bright moon lit her way. When she stepped down onto the beach, she glanced around. It was a beautiful early morning. She could easily make out the waves, and found the task of agate dropping much easier than she had the night before.

In fact, she found herself enjoying the walk along the beach. Alone with Mother Nature, she felt a curious kinship. She paused briefly to stare out at the ocean. When a powerful wave came in, it was only when she felt the water wash across her feet that she leapt back in an awkward high-step.

She resumed her task and soon reached the dune. She checked her pack and found she had several agates left, and wondered, should she drop additional agates on her return trip? Deciding she might as well, she started back. She was just about back to her grandmother's home when she heard voices on the beach.

She glanced around frantically, and then made a mad dash for the sandy hillside. She planted herself against it, intently scanning the beach. The voices sounded as if they were close, but when she spotted a couple of teenagers stepping down an embankment off the parking lot, she realized the wind had carried their voices. But what were they doing on the beach at this time of night? It was against town rules.

Deciding she wouldn't stick around to find out, she stealthily climbed the hill up to her grandmother's lawn. From there, she turned to watch the teenagers for a moment. Fortunately, they turned and began walking back up the embankment to the parking lot. Had they seen her? She hoped not.

When she stepped through the front door of her grandmother's house, Mary watched her expectantly. "Did it go all right?"

"Great, other than I nearly ran into a couple teenagers."

"Did they see you?"

Paige shook her head. "Hard to say, but if they did, they didn't let on. I have to wonder what a couple of kids were doing out this early in the morning. What's up with parents these days? What's up with kids these days?"

Mary chuckled. "Every generation says that, you know?"

"You're probably right." Paige shed the backpack and her coat, and then returned the pepper spray and stun gun to the drawer in the kitchen. "What time is it, Gram?"

"It's a little after four. You made excellent time. Are you going back to bed?"

Paige considered the question. "I think I'll get a shower and stay up. I'm feeling fairly alert."

By mid-morning, however, she was feeling anything but alert, and when she woke to Wyatt standing over her as she lay on the couch, she colored under his gaze. A contemplative look shaded his features.

"You know, sweetheart, most people come to the beach to recharge their batteries," he said, "and generally, the sea air invigorates and refreshes them. I'm afraid it's killing you."

"Oh, it is not," she scoffed as she sat up. "I'm just tired, that's all."

"Why?" he asked crisply.

She ignored his question. "How are you?" she asked instead. Suddenly, she remembered the accident at the South Hole. "Gram said you've been busy investigating the accident."

"Deflecting again," he murmured, but let it slide. "Yeah, tragically, a sixteen-year-old kid went off the road."

"Oh, no—did he miss the detour signs?"

"No," Wyatt said, frowning. "His friends tell me they were playing a game of chicken, seeing how close each could speed his car toward the crevasse without actually going into it."

Paige's hand flew to her mouth.

"Kids that age think they're invincible," Wyatt said sadly.

Paige nodded. "Have you eaten? I can make you something."

"No, that's okay. I've had lunch. I'm going home—to my real home," he clarified. "I've got work to do, sorting out the accident, and with all the parties involved, it could take weeks. I'll be back and forth between here and there for a while."

"Wyatt, that's awful. So you'll be stuck driving that detour often?"

"I'm afraid so," he said.

Paige rose from the couch and stretched her stiffened muscles. Wyatt noticed her wince from the muscle pain throughout her body.

"Paige, are you all right? Should you think about seeing a doctor?"

Although she was warmed by his concern, she couldn't tell him she was simply sore from the exertion of a strenuous nightly workout. "I'm fine, Wy. Really."

When he stepped forward and pulled her into his arms, her heart gave an erratic thump. She hadn't expected his embrace, but she melted against him.

He kissed the top of her head, and then spoke into her ear. "You never said how long you intend to stay this time . . ."

He trailed off, and she felt him stiffen in anticipation of her response. She couldn't give him an answer. Variables, each beyond her control, dictated the duration of her visit. "I'll stay . . . as long as I can," she said. It was the best she could give him.

He nodded crisply and pulled back. "I'll call you."

"Operation Save Agate Cove is a success! Well, so far," Jeanette said cheerfully, as she dangled the newspaper in front of her friends' faces. She dropped it on the tabletop.

The whole group was present, sitting around the dinette in Mary's kitchen. Paige reached for the paper first. On the front page, Jeanette's freckle-faced grandson Davy smiled at her, his outstretched hands overflowing with agates.

"Oh, he really is adorable," Paige murmured. "Just look at those freckles."

"I imagine Wyatt had freckles when he was a kid," Mary observed.

Paige ignored the remark. "Okay, we made the paper—er, the little redheaded cutie made the paper—but we can't call a victory yet."

"Oh, but"—Jeanette grinned, leaning forward in her chair— "my friend from Portland called, and she told me we made the paper there. I guess piles of beautiful agates showing up on a beach, when they've been conspicuously absent for years, makes headlines."

"Lucky for us," Dori mused as she took the paper from Paige. "Oh, he is such a cute little boy. Look at all that red hair."

"Okay," Mary said with authority, "we all agree Davy is adorable, but let's talk." She rose from the table, ignoring her crutches propped against her chair, and pulled several sheets of paper off the kitchen counter. "Okay, girls, here's the up-dated agate-drop schedule." She passed each woman a sheet. Each studied it for a moment or two.

"Oh, well, uh," Jeanette said, clearing her throat, "I'm not sure if this day, well, and this one," she pointed to a couple of her assigned shifts, "will work for me."

Dori grimaced. "Oh, my, I see several conflicts for me too."

"I'm afraid I do too," Minnie said apologetically.

Mary harrumphed in disgust. "Girls, saving our town must be our priority, or our town *will* die. And Paige cannot carry this load alone."

"But . . . ," Jeanette said.

"No buts," Mary said firmly. "If you can't do your assigned shift, then it's up to you to have someone else cover for you. The important thing is that we make our agate drops every night until we see positive results for this town."

"Gram, shouldn't we slow down some—at least until the tourists start coming in numbers?" Paige asked. "I've already covered the beach with agates. Maybe we won't have to make the drops every morning."

"The locals have been taking the agates," Minnie pointed out. "The sand is picked clean almost every day."

Mary nodded. "We have to keep that sand covered. And we'll have to increase the numbers of agates on the beach as the tourists come. It's all about supply and demand."

Paige watched her curiously. "Maybe we should hold back distributing too many agates," she said, "until we know if tourists are even coming."

"Oh, they'll come," Mary said with certainty. "And I'll be sure we have enough agates to keep the beach covered for the whole summer, but since we're still early in our venture, and with the North and South holes creating such a headache, I'd like to assure that any tourists who do make the trek here— you know, who do the detour—are rewarded for their efforts."

"Oh," Paige said, "okay, I guess. You've really been thinking this out, Gram."

"It's what I do. I think." She tossed an angry look at her foot. "It's not as if I can do much else."

Chapter Ten

Paige saw little of Wyatt over the next three weeks. He stopped by occasionally to retrieve something from the apartment, or to visit with her and Mary briefly, always during the day, and then he was off to tend to his work south of the South Hole. Paige noticed he was looking as fatigued as he claimed she looked.

Although she missed Wyatt, and was saddened by his reasons for having to be away, she had to admit that having him gone made Operation Save Agate Cove easier to carry out. Without him hovering, watchful of her every move, she could go about her business more readily.

She was definitely feeling the fatigue of Operation Save Agate Cove, however. While each of the ladies took their occasional shift, none was doing her promised part in the endeavor. As much as Paige hated to harp on their lack of commitment, she needed help. She had performed the agate drops three of the last four nights, and she was desperate for a break. Every time one of the ladies couldn't complete her shift, she called Paige to cover, knowing full well she wouldn't say no.

"Gram," Paige said as the two sat down to dinner, "Dori is going to do the drop tonight, right?"

Mary winced, and Paige understood immediately that Dori was dropping the ball once again. She sighed loudly. "Gram, what's up with her? I can't keep covering for her and the other two when they aren't able to show up. They made the same commitment I did."

Mary shook her head crisply. "It's true, they did. And I'm sorry they're not holding up their parts of the bargain." She reached across the table and took Paige's hand. "Honey, do you want to forget this? I'd understand if you do. I'm so sorry I'm unable to do my part."

Paige shook her head with a long sigh. "No, I don't want to stop. It's working, Gram. That's the thing. After all those newspapers picked up the story, tourists started flooding in. In fact, I think we're going to need to order more agates off the *Television Shopping Show* soon."

"We are running close to empty," Mary observed. "But I placed an order two weeks ago. I got a call yesterday, and the agates are waiting for us in Portland. Jeanette promised she'd pick them up tomorrow."

"I'll see it to believe it," Paige murmured doubtfully.

Mary glanced at Paige tentatively. "Honey, can you manage the drop tonight? Jeanette promises me she'll cover it tomorrow. And I promise you that I'll be calling Dori this evening to give her a talking-to. I get that she's afraid to be out on the beach alone, but you're doing it, and so is Jeanette and Minnie—well, they do it occasionally, anyway."

Paige saw the anguish in her grandmother's eyes. She knew the older woman was worrying herself sick about her. While she was out on the beach, making her agate drop, Mary waited at home, wringing her hands nervously and staring out the front window. She saw the relief in her grandmother's eyes every time she returned home safely.

"I'll do the drop, Gram. Heck, my body has never been in better shape, from all the walking and climbing. If I wasn't so tired, I'd probably be feeling great."

Mary smiled sadly. "That's the spirit, honey."

Around three o'clock in the morning, Paige stepped onto the sandy beach. A swirling mist caressed her face, but she was relieved to see that the light fog didn't significantly obstruct her view of the beach. She walked along, tossing the agates onto the wet sand, and enjoying the swishing sounds of the waves. The ocean was relatively calm by Oregon coast standards, and she found herself relaxing courtesy of the gentle sounds around her.

The feeling was short-lived, however. As she walked the stretch back to her grandmother's property, she heard laughter on the beach. She glanced over her left shoulder and spotted a group of people jogging down the embankment and onto the sand, arms laden with chairs, coolers, and blankets.

What were they doing down here this early in the morning? she wondered angrily. The beach was closed between dusk and six A.M.

She winced when she realized she was currently on the beach during prohibited hours, but she was there for a good cause. With relief, she realized the group of revelers hadn't noticed her, and she dropped down low and made a run toward the trail. Unfortunately, two of the men in the group ran full-out toward her.

Her heart lodged in her throat. She sank to her knees and tugged the stun gun from her pocket. She crawled into the scraggly shrubs and waited in readiness for them, the stun gun poised in front of her. She took deep breaths of the ocean air in an attempt to slow her pounding heart.

One of the men was suddenly so close that she could touch him, but oddly, he made no move toward her. She almost laughed with relief when she heard the thunk of a Frisbee hitting his hand. She knew then that he hadn't seen her. She felt ridiculous for her suspicions, but then felt frustrated when the two continued their game so close to where she was hiding.

On it went for thirty minutes or so, the glow-in-the-dark sphere making an early-morning game possible, and Paige wondered grimly if it was going to go on forever. At one point, the Frisbee landed near the breaking waves. A young man clad in shorts bent to pick it up, but paused, overlooking the wet sand. "Hey, look at these!" he shouted to his friend. "Look at all these rocks."

His Frisbee partner jogged over to him, and the two stared with bent heads over the agates. "They're agates, and they're everywhere," the first man said, glancing around.

"Oh, yeah," the second man said. "I read about these. It's why Kate insisted on coming here. She loves beachcombing."

"Let's finish our game," the first said, "and then we'll get the girls and do a little beachcombing before the other tourists get here. After driving that crazy road here, we might as well leave with something for our trouble."

So, the newspaper coverage was definitely working, Paige thought. She wondered if the local businesses were noticing an increase in customers, and suspected they were. They had to be. The public beach seemed to come more alive with tourists with each passing day.

Paige's thoughts and eyes were drawn back to the young men, who jogged across the sand and resumed their game. Paige rolled her eyes. This was ridiculous. Where was law enforcement when you needed them? Surely someone should be policing this beach. And then she grinned sheepishly. She knew full well why no one was policing the beach, and that it was a good thing for her sake.

When the Frisbee suddenly sailed her way, high above one

of the young mens' heads, he dove for it, hitting the sand with his shoulder and causing a spray of sand to cover Paige's head and face. Fortunately, the kid didn't see her, and Paige managed to force back a sputter from her lips.

The sand went everywhere—in her eyes, nose, and mouth. Some had even gone down the front of her shirt. She couldn't keep her hands from flying to her eyes. She was careful not to rub them, but blinked gently in an effort to dislodge the gritty grains. It was no use. She'd have to deal with it later.

With a sigh, she sank back against the sand, since she couldn't go anywhere now. She dozed off, but finally started awake when a seagull shrieked nearby. To her horror, it was light outside. She blinked against the bright sunlight, attempting to focus. A quick glance down the beach confirmed beachcombers had already started their searches for agate treasure. The Frisbee players were long gone.

Paige rolled over onto her knees, her stiffened muscles protesting the exertion. She rose up with a groan and then started up the steep hill. When she reached the top, she was mortified to see Wyatt standing at the western end of the property, behind the low fence, staring out over the ocean. She promptly dropped to her knees behind the crest of the hill and hoped he hadn't seen her out of the corner of his eye.

Since he didn't turn her way, she reasoned he had not, and she rose up ever so slightly to cast a glance at the front of her grandmother's house. It was no surprise to see her grandmother's worried face pressed against the glass of the door. Paige offered a tiny wave, which her grandmother returned with an utterly relieved expression on her face.

Unfortunately, Wyatt turned then, spotted Mary behind the glass, followed her gaze, and saw Paige before she could drop back down onto the sand. He watched her, mouth agape, and then strode toward her with an expression of horror.

She rose up and offered a sickly smile. "Hi, Wy."

"Paige, what are you doing over there?" he demanded. He reached out with both hands, took her arms, and hauled her to her feet. Wyatt's face still registered shock. He tipped his face to the side to study her, and took note of the sand and debris all over her hair, face, and clothing. He shook his head in confusion. "Were you lying on the sand?" he asked, still shaking his head in puzzlement. "Were you hiding from me, Paige?"

"Of course I wasn't! I was, uh, taking a walk, and I fell . . ."

"You fell? Are you all right?" He studied her face, arms, and legs again for evidence of injury.

"I'm fine," she assured him, "just a little . . . sandy. Hey, you're back. For how long?"

He hesitated before answering. "I got back late last night. Paige, it's six-fifteen in the morning. I'm worried about you. Every time I call, you're sleeping. And now I find you up early, covered with sand and looking like death."

"I look like death?" she asked, failing to mask the hurt. Wyatt thought she looked like death? Well, if she did, it wasn't her fault.

"Paige, you're beautiful, but you look . . . awful. Your eyes are all puffy and swollen . . ." He stepped back for a better look. "I don't think there's an inch of you that isn't covered with sand."

"Was that supposed to make me feel better?" she demanded.

He leveled his gaze at her. "I'm taking you to a doctor."

"You are not!" she said, aghast. "I've never been healthier in my life."

He raised both hands with a weary sigh. "I'll tell you what. You are going to bed if I have to put you there myself."

"Oh, no you won't. I'm a grown woman, perfectly capable of deciding when to sleep and when to stay awake."

Wyatt sighed heavily. "Paige, I don't want to fight with you.

I'm beat too. Why don't you get some sleep and we can talk later? Look, let's have lunch together after you have a nap."

His conciliatory tone went a long way toward soothing her anger—probably because she was too tired to argue. "You didn't say—are you home for good?" she asked. "I mean, are you *here* to stay for a while?"

He scrubbed a hand over his jaw. "Yeah, I'm back for a while. I've completed the investigation into the traffic homicide at the South Hole, so now it's up to the Prosecutor's Office to decide what to do."

Paige nodded and turned to walk to the house. Wyatt fell into step beside her and took her arm. She nearly shrugged out of his grasp, but couldn't deny he was essentially keeping her upright.

Inside the house, they found Mary in the foyer, forcing a cheerful smile. "How was your walk on the beach, Paige?"

Wyatt harrumphed in disgust. "Does she look like she did much walking? She's wearing half the sand from that beach."

"Oh, I am not," Paige harrumphed this time. "I had a wonderful walk. It's glorious to commune with nature, to feel the gentle breeze, and listen to the waves . . ."

"Gentle breeze!" Wyatt scoffed. "It's really windy out there," he said. "According to the weather report, we've been having forty-mile-an-hour wind gusts for the last hour."

How had she missed that important detail? Paige wondered. Lord, she really must be tired. "Just the same, I can't get enough of Mother Nature," she insisted.

"Looks like you got to know Mother Nature real well," Wyatt observed drolly, reaching to brush sand off her cheek. "It looks like she threw sand in your face."

"I'm going to bed." Paige started off, but stopped. "First, I'm taking a shower." She started off again, but in the opposite direction of the bathroom.

Wyatt reached out to take hold of her arm and turned her around. "Isn't the bathroom that way?"

"That it is," she murmured sheepishly. "But I think I'd better go outside and wipe off as much of this sand as I can before I get in the shower. I'm getting it all over the floor as we stand here."

She headed outside and Wyatt followed. She braced against the wind and started slapping off the sand. Wyatt attempted to help by gently dusting the sand off her arms and face. When he reached a warm hand to her throat and gently dusted the sand off her neck, she found him far too distracting. She grasped his hand and smiled self-consciously into his eyes. "I . . . got it, Wy."

He grinned sheepishly this time. "I was just trying to help. It's what I do."

She didn't miss the sparkle of humor in his blue eyes. "Uh-huh," she said.

He flashed a mischievous smile and pulled her into his arms. He held her close for a long moment and she gave a sleepy sigh of contentment.

"I missed you," he said.

"I missed you too."

He pulled back, his gaze sweeping over her face. He reached a gentle finger to her eyelashes, attempting to carefully brush away the stubborn grains of sand. When his thumb trailed across her lips, she pulled away. "I should get inside."

She headed back into the house and toward the bathroom. Wyatt followed her inside, but paused in the foyer. Mary, who was waiting for them there, made as if to leave too. Wyatt gently took hold of her arm. "I think it's time we had a little chat, my friend," he said. "Don't you?"

"Well, you know I always enjoy our little chats, Wyatt," Mary said agreeably.

Chapter Eleven

If Wyatt thinks he can break me, he has another think coming," Mary said angrily. "That boy's charm doesn't work on me. I'll tell you that much. I ought to take him out behind the woodshed."

Paige heard the tail end of her grandmother's phone conversation as she stepped into the room. No doubt Mary was referring to Wyatt's attempt at interrogating her, while she had been sleeping off the effects of her early-morning adventure.

"Jeanette, I have to go. Paige is awake." Mary was silent for a moment. "I know. Yes, I know. *I know.*"

"Gram, what's up with Jeanette?" Paige asked with interest, as she sank into the plush cushions of the couch.

Mary averted her gaze briefly, but then turned back to Paige and met her eyes full-on. "She can't make the drive to Portland to pick up the rocks. When she told Ralph she intended to drive the detour, he had a fit—said it wasn't safe. Yada, yada, yada," she intoned angrily. "Paige, how are we going to save this town if my friends don't do their parts? I'm becoming so frustrated."

Mary fell back into her recliner and cast an angry glance at her foot. "I am so sick and tired of this injury. I should be helping you, instead of sitting here with my leg up like some weak-kneed little princess."

"Hey, Gram," Paige said with a smile. "Your knees are fine. It's the foot that's the problem, and I'm just glad you don't need surgery. You will, and I mean *will,* stay off that foot until it heals properly."

When Paige heard Mary sniffle and saw her wipe at her eyes, she hurriedly rose from the couch to wrap a comforting arm around her shoulders. "Gram, don't be upset. Everything is going to be all right."

"Paige, you can't keep carrying the load for everyone. You've taken almost full responsibility for Operation Save Agate Cove, and . . . you don't even live heeerrreeee."

Mary burst into tears, something Paige had never seen her stalwart grandmother do. It broke her heart.

"Gram, please don't cry. Everything is fine. We'll get through this. The road will soon open up again on both ends, and then the agate drops will stop. Until then, you can count on me."

"Honey, I've always been able to count on you."

"And you always will. I'll drive to Portland for the rocks."

Mary's expression looked stricken at the idea of Paige driving to Portland by herself. "I'm going with you," she said resolutely.

"You will not. You can't ride all that way with your foot on the floor, and I don't know how we'd manage to keep it raised in the cab of the truck. No, Gram, we're not taking any chances."

"Honey, you're too tired to drive to Portland."

"I agree." Wyatt stepped into the room, wearing a grim expression on his face.

The two women glanced at one another with alarm. *How much of their conversation had Wyatt heard?*

"What's this talk about Paige driving to Portland? What possible reason do you have for needing to drive to Portland?" Wyatt's eyes flashed.

Okay, good, Paige thought with relief. He obviously hadn't heard any mention of the rocks.

"You do know that detour is treacherous, particularly when you don't know these roads," he said fiercely.

"I drove it, Wyatt. Remember?" Paige said.

"Yeah, one time." He turned away from her and looked at Mary. "You're not going to let her go, are you?"

Mary shrugged helplessly. *They needed those agates. What else could they do?*

"I'll drive," he said stiffly. "I'll be waiting in my truck."

"Wyatt," Paige called after him. "I'm not even ready yet."

"Well, get ready."

Paige glanced at Mary, who nodded. "Go—Wyatt will keep you safe."

"Gram, I don't need anyone keeping me safe," she said in a fatigued voice. "I'm a grown woman."

"Okay, you keep him safe then."

Paige laughed grimly. "Will do."

Paige appeared beside the driver's-side door of Wyatt's truck. He wearily rolled down the window.

"I'll drive," she said.

"Right," he said with a laugh. "It'll be a minor miracle if you manage to stay awake until we reach the cutoff to the detour."

"Is that a challenge, Wy?

"No, it's not. Get in the truck."

"Really, Wy, I can drive."

"Paige, get in. Go to sleep, please. God knows, you need rest."

She climbed into the truck and turned toward him. "Wyatt, why are you so concerned about me?"

He shoved the keys into the ignition and pressed the gas. "Because I love you," he said gruffly, as the truck surged forward. "I always have."

Paige sat quietly in the truck as they drove toward the detour. She didn't respond to Wyatt's declaration. It took her by surprise. She cast a hesitant glance at his angry profile. She saw a muscle working in his jaw, and realized he was having trouble maintaining his composure.

She knew she should say something in return, but couldn't bring herself to say those three words back. *I love you.*

Those words necessitated action on her part, a willingness to drop her defenses, and she knew *those* words, spoken aloud, would force decisions she simply couldn't make right now. There wasn't time to make them—decisions that both deserved and required her full attention.

No, she had too much on her plate right now. She had a town to save, and that reality necessitated that she keep some measure of distance between her and local law enforcement—Wyatt. She had to protect him—to keep him in the dark about her early-morning activities—at least until the roads opened.

But she had to say something . . .

"Wy, I appreciate you driving me to Portland. You really didn't have to, you know."

He turned toward her then, watched her briefly through narrowed eyes, and then turned back to the road. When he turned left onto the detour road, she took another stab at making amends. "Really, Wy, why don't you let me drive? I know you're tired."

He pulled off to the side of the road and turned to face her. "You want to drive? Really—you think you're up for driving?" He shook his head. "Something is going on with you, and I want to help. But you won't let me. Paige, you're frustrating the heck out of me. Don't you trust me?"

"Wyatt," she said soothingly, "yes, I trust you. And, Wy, I don't need help."

"I guess you don't need me, then."

Her anguished eyes bored into his.

"Are you driving or what, Paige?"

"No," she said with a beleaguered sigh.

"That's a good answer."

Wyatt pulled onto the narrow roadway. Just as Paige remembered, this road was like a roller coaster, and if she was driving, she realized she would likely be white-knuckling the steering wheel. Wyatt, on the other hand, knew the road well and his driving posture had relaxed—somewhat.

The two rode in silence, with Paige staring out the passenger-side window. She only looked Wyatt's way when she heard him slip in a CD. The music was soft and lilting, and the last thing she needed to hear when she was on the brink of exhaustion. She reached a slender finger toward the CD player and ejected it. Wyatt shot her an angry look and slipped it back in.

"That music will make you tired," she told him.

"No, it'll make *you* tired. So why don't you go to sleep?"

Paige gave an angry snort and turned away from him. She stared out at the passing scenery, mesmerized by the myriad hues of green in the Pacific Northwest forest. This really was beautiful country.

Soon, the whir of the scenery caused her to feel sleepy, and she shook her head. She found her eyelids growing heavy, but she started awake when she heard, and felt, her head clunk against the window. She raised a hand to the lump currently erupting on the side of her head.

She glanced at Wyatt with alarm, and then her eyes narrowed angrily when he gave her an I-told-you-so smile.

She turned away from him but glanced back when he

pulled off the road. "Are you going to let me drive?" she asked.

"Oh, sure," he muttered sarcastically. "I have a death wish." He reached toward her, unbuckled her seatbelt, and then hauled her against him.

"What are you doing?" she demanded.

"Trying to help you get some sleep," he said.

"I'm fine, Wy," she said with a yawn.

He met her gaze. She saw no flashing anger—only concern, and a curious resignation. He leaned toward her and skimmed his cheek against hers. "Try to rest," he said softly, and then draped a protective arm over her shoulder. He shifted the truck into drive and resumed the drive to I-5.

Pressed against him, and so tired, Paige found herself drifting off to sleep. She simply couldn't fight it anymore— or him—not at this particular moment. *Why would she want to?* she wondered fleetingly, sleepily. She loved him—had always loved him. And it was all right now. They were both adults. She snuggled against him. *This moment, it was all right.*

"Go to sleep, Paige," he said.

"I love you, Wy," she murmured. "I always have."

Paige woke up to the sound of gravel crunching under the truck tires. She glanced up, blinking, and rubbed her eyes. She was sure there was still sand lodged in them.

"Don't rub them," Wyatt warned, "or the sand might scratch your cornea and do real damage." He sighed loudly and worriedly at the prospect.

"Where are we?" she asked.

"It's after one. Are you hungry?"

She glanced up to see that he had pulled up to a fast-food restaurant. She nodded and climbed out of the truck. He met her at the passenger door and took her hand. Together they walked into the restaurant.

"What sounds good to you?" Wyatt asked.

"Oh, anything," she said, glad Wyatt seemed in better spirits. Earlier, he'd been so frustrated with her.

He nodded and walked to the counter to place their order, while she seated herself at a booth. He returned and sat across from her.

"How far are we from Portland?" Paige asked.

"About an hour and fifteen minutes away. We'll get on I-5, and then it's a straight shot into downtown."

Paige nodded and glanced around to take in their surroundings. Wyatt rose to retrieve their order when their number was called. She watched him walk away. He definitely looked good in the jeans that hugged his muscular legs, and when he turned carrying a tray of food, she nearly swooned at the sight of the polo shirt stretched across his broad chest.

"Are you checking me out?" he asked with a grin. "If I didn't know better, I'd think you were admiring my form."

She laughed, not bothering to deny it. When he put the tray on the table, she scanned the contents. He had remembered her favorite foods. He'd ordered her a cheeseburger, fries, and a chocolate shake. He'd ordered himself the same burger and fries, but preferred a vanilla shake.

Paige smiled absently, remembering how often they'd shared meals together as young adults. Often they'd driven into Lincoln City, and sometimes on to Newport. They'd had so much fun together.

Wyatt noticed the wistful smile on her face. "What are you thinking about?" he asked.

She chuckled self-consciously. "I was just remembering all the fun we used to have together."

He reached across the table and took her hand. His earnest

eyes sought hers. "It's like I said before, Paige—it's as if time has stood still." He pulled back and raked a hand through his hair. "It's probably pretty clear to you now, I'd like to . . ."

"You'd like to do what, Wy?"

He glanced away, and then back. "I'd like to pick up where we left off. Like I said, it's like . . . we never . . . left off." He smiled self-consciously now. "Does it feel that way to you?"

She nodded. "Yes, it does."

"So, let's do it," he said. "Let's pick up exactly where we left off."

"And where exactly did we leave off?"

He grinned ruefully. "Well, we left off with me being a stupid kid, trying to talk you into marrying me, and . . . you having the good sense to say no."

The admission took her by surprise. "You were so angry with me back then, Wyatt, but I just couldn't make the same mistakes my mother did." She shook her head. "My mother married so young, and look how that worked for her. I used to worry, what if I was more like her than I was willing to admit? What if, somewhere deep within me, I was reckless like her, and ultimately caused the same kind of pain?"

"Paige, you're nothing like your mother."

She shook her head, fighting back tears. "I just couldn't do it, to you, to Dad, to Gram—even to her."

"I know." He smiled. "You made the right choice. It was reason enough to say no because we *were* just kids. You were far more adult than me, because you were determined that each of us experience enough of life to make the right choices. I remember your words: 'If our love is true, it will survive time and distance.' "

"But you were so hurt and angry."

"Angry? Not really. Hurt at the time, yes." He weighed his response. "Yeah, okay, I was angry—then." He stroked his jaw, and then shook his head. "No, wait. It wasn't anger. I could never be angry with you—well, not for long anyway. I was . . . afraid—afraid I was losing you forever. Frankly, Paige, I count it a minor miracle I haven't lost you." He flashed a quick, hopeful grin. "I haven't, have I?"

She smiled. What could she say? *Hey, Wy, I know you have feelings for me, and me for you, but could we kind of hold off for a while?* But in answer to his question she said, "No, Wy. You haven't lost me. We've found one another again, and I am . . ."

"What?"

"I'm so happy about that."

He seemed to sigh with relief.

"What is it, Wy?"

"I was half-afraid you were going to tell me you didn't love me."

She glanced away. She knew she hadn't said the words. Had she hurt him by her silence?

"I happen to know you do love me," he said with a glimmer of humor in his eyes.

Her eyes shot to his and she lowered her brows questioningly.

"You talk in your sleep," he told her with a broad grin.

"I do?"

"Yep—and if I listen carefully enough, I'm thinking you might say something that might very well be a clue as to what you, your grandmother, and your friends are up to."

"Don't count on it," she murmured.

"So, you admit you're involved in something you . . . shouldn't be?"

"No, I do not!"

Wyatt studied her face. "Paige, I don't want to upset you with what I'm about to say, but I know in my gut you are hiding something from me, and it does scare me."

"So all that ridiculous teasing you do masks your fear," she said with a sympathetic laugh.

"Yes," he said seriously. "On the one hand, I sense you have strong feelings for me—that you're open to a relationship—but on the other hand, you're not telling me . . . something."

This time Paige weighed her response carefully. "If that were true, it . . . would be because I'd want to protect you. And if it *were* true, I'd—I'd ask you to give me a little time."

"And how much time would you ask for—if say, hypothetically, you needed this time?"

She shrugged. "If I needed this time, it would probably mean that—whatever situation I was dealing with—would likely be over by summer's end, if indeed I was dealing with . . . something. Would that be okay with you?"

Wyatt watched her speculatively. "Sweetheart, it's been ten years. I think I can manage a couple of months. But why?" He comically stroked his jaw as if he were a detective sleuthing some hidden truth, but then he sobered. "Frankly, Paige, you are scaring me, and I am worried about you. You want to protect me, but I'm a big boy. I can take care of myself." He eyed her thoughtfully. "You are clearly exhausted, and clearly up to something. But . . . I'll give you all the time you need, because I love you."

"Wyatt, I'm just asking that you trust me."

He leaned back in his seat. "I can do that."

As Paige reached for a french fry and popped it into her mouth, she wondered, *Could he? Could he manage to trust her until Operation Save Agate Cove ended?*

Chapter Twelve

Wyatt steered his truck into the industrial complex near downtown Portland. Paige consulted the slip of paper with the address Mary had given her. "It's over there," Paige told him, pointing at a large, open bay—one of many running the length of a large, concrete building.

He nodded and drove into an adjacent parking lot. Paige dropped out of the truck and climbed a few steps to where a man with a clipboard waited for her. She passed him a paper identifying the items she was picking up. He glanced at the sheet and nodded. "Be right back," he said cheerfully.

"Thanks!" Paige called after him.

Suddenly, Paige's eyes widened with concern. What if the boxed agates were clearly marked as such? She tried to remember. Had the boxes at her grandmother's been labeled? She simply couldn't remember, and was on pins and needles with anticipation. If the boxes were labeled, there would be no way she could keep her secret from Wyatt any longer.

The man reappeared and called out to Wyatt, who stood

with one hand on the sidewall of the truck. "You can back the truck up here."

Wyatt hopped into the truck and easily backed it into the narrow space. The man with the clipboard passed it to Paige along with a pen. She signed for the boxes, and then stood back as two men began loading them into the truck. Wyatt took a step forward to help, but the apparent boss of the crew waved him away. "We'll take care of it," he called. "Liability, and all that—you know how it is."

Wyatt nodded and stepped back beside Paige, who noted with absolute relief that the boxes weren't labeled but simply showed the warehouse's address. Paige suspected her grandmother had been adamant that the boxes remain clear of any conspicuous labeling.

Paige practically jumped when Wyatt draped an arm over her shoulder. "Look," he said, his eyes narrowed suspiciously, "twelve more 'private' boxes. I wonder what's in them?"

Paige shrugged. "Who knows?"

"Oh, I think you know."

Paige wagged a finger at him. "Remember the importance of trust."

Wyatt gave her a quick hug, and then jumped into the bed of the truck to assure that the boxes were stowed safely for the trip back to Agate Cove. Paige wasn't surprised when he hefted one to gauge the weight. "These things are heavy, Paige! You didn't lift this, did you?"

"The boxes I carried weren't particularly heavy," she lied.

Wyatt looked skeptical, but apparently decided to take her answer at face value. Soon, the couple was back in the truck for the long drive back to Agate Cove. As they left Portland via a massive span of concrete bridge, Paige glanced over at the city skyline. "I always thought Portland was a pretty city," she observed.

Wyatt nodded. "I lived here for a while—I took a job with

the Feds right out of college, and I spent some time here training. I like the area, but could do without the rain."

"Hey, it rains all the time at Agate Cove," Paige pointed out.

"Yes, but there I have the ocean to look at."

"True," she acknowledged. "What kind of work did you do, specifically?" she asked. "And do not make the joke that if you tell me, you'll have to kill me."

Wyatt remained quiet, and she cast him a curious glance. He shrugged in response.

"You *really* can't tell me?"

"Nope."

"Sounds dangerous," she said.

He didn't answer, but instead changed the subject. "When we get back to Mary's, I'll help you get those *private* boxes inside. I don't want you lifting them."

"Your concern is sweet, but I'm perfectly capable of lifting a box a few inches onto a hand truck."

"So that's how you moved them so quickly before. Just let me move them, please."

She decided to change the subject. "Are you happy to be living back at Agate Cove?" She smiled sheepishly. "That's kind of a stupid question, isn't it? In light of the fact that you're not actually living in your own home right now. I imagine you'd like nothing better than to get back to your own place. It must be a nightmare being cut off from all your stuff."

He shrugged. "Oh, I don't know. Living at your grandmother's has its perks." He grinned at her and took her hand.

"I wonder why Gram didn't mention to me that you were staying with her when she asked me to come."

"She probably thought you wouldn't come if she did."

"Why would you say that?"

"*Would* you have come? My guess is no. You would have worried about how awkward it would be to see me again, let alone live on the same property together."

"Hey, Wy, I was glad to see you—admittedly a little stunned—but you didn't look especially pleased to see me that first time," she reminded him.

Wyatt chuckled. "You know, you're the only person who has ever shortened my name like that. But anyway, in response to what you just said, it wasn't that I was angry. I was in shock. First, before I even realized it *was* you, I watched you very nearly meet your Maker, and then, when I knew it was you, the fact that you had very nearly met your Maker nearly caused *me* to meet my Maker. I think you cost me ten years of my life. You'd better spend the next fifty making it up to me."

"Ah, you care," she teased, but then his last sentence registered. *Did he just say what she thought he had said?*

"You think so? Of course I care! By the way, move over here, but be careful when you do it."

She quickly unbuckled her seatbelt and scooted closer to him. "Belt back up," he said, glancing at her quickly and then back to the road. Once she was strapped in beside him, he draped an arm over her shoulder.

They drove in silence for a minute. Without turning to see her face, Wyatt broke the silence. "It really is as if we never parted. It's like all's right with my world again. It's a curious feeling of déjà vu. I wonder, are most couples able to pick up where they left off like this? You know, Paige, I have loved you from the moment I set eyes on you."

"That's sweet, Wy." She smiled and said, "Me too."

The two left Portland behind and merged onto I-5. As Wyatt steered along the major highway, he talked a lot about his past, but without being overly specific. Paige learned that he had lived in Portland for a year, and had then been transferred to Washington D.C., where he had worked for Homeland Security until just recently.

"Can I ask you something?"

"Sure, what is it?"

"Why did you give up your job? I remember when we were kids, you talked a lot about wanting to work for the Federal Bureau of Investigation. Even if you didn't go that particular route, it sounds as if you chose a similar road with Homeland Security."

He nodded and glanced at her briefly, before turning back to the road. "I guess I did achieve what I set out to," he acknowledged, "but it . . . didn't make me happy."

Paige pondered his answer for a moment. She remembered his father had worked in law enforcement all his life, holding a prestigious position, though Paige had never known specifically what he did either.

"Did you choose the law enforcement route because you were following in your father's footsteps?" Paige asked.

Wyatt considered the question. "Not really—although Dad sure wasn't happy when I left the job. He really let me have it." Wyatt laughed without mirth. "He accused me of throwing my life away. No, I'm in law enforcement because it's what I want, but where Dad and I differ is where we want to *do* the job."

Paige nodded, and Wyatt continued. "The irony is, Dad wants to be a big fish in a big pond, but I just want to *live* by the biggest pond of all—the Pacific Ocean. I like small-town life. I refuse to apologize for that, and my dad will either have to accept it or not. It's his choice."

"I feel a similar pull to the ocean," Paige commented. "I guess that's why the only places I've lived in my life were both on the Pacific Ocean."

Wyatt aimed a finger ahead. "There's the detour." He pulled off the freeway and steered toward the narrow road that Paige found herself dreading.

"I'm glad I'm not driving," she admitted.

"Well, it's big of you to finally admit it," he teased.

"But I will drive if you want me to."

"I've got it covered."

Wyatt pulled up to a convenience store. "I'm going to grab a coffee. You want one?"

She shook her head no.

While Wyatt was in the store, Paige pulled a folded newspaper from between the truck seats. Dated that day, it showed a large photo of colorful agates spread out over the public beach at Agate Cove, with the headline reading: "Scientists Attribute Abundance of Agates to Natural Phenomenon."

Paige's eyes widened in surprise. She felt a sense of panic descending over her. While she'd known the agates would cause a stir, she had certainly never believed that oceanographers and geologists would take an interest in them. She scanned the article, becoming sicker with dread by the second. Apparently two world-renowned oceanographers, as well as a noted geologist, intended to visit the beach the following week.

Paige felt a sudden wave of nausea. She took a deep steadying breath, trying to stave off the panic. When Wyatt opened the door and climbed in beside her, she attempted a smile, but couldn't quite pull it off.

He noticed the paper on her lap and tapped the picture of the agates with his finger. "Isn't that something?" he said. "Since I was so busy investigating the fatality over at the South Hole, I've been out of the loop. I guess the return of those agates to the beach is sparking national interest—even international interest."

Paige gulped.

"Apparently scientists are especially intrigued, since agates typically show up between October and April—when they do show up, that is. Agates have been missing from our beach for many years."

"Really?" Paige said numbly. "That's interesting." It was interesting, all right, she thought. It was June now. Why hadn't her grandmother or any one of her friends known that agates had a season of sorts? And that season was essentially over.

"Yeah, it is interesting," Wyatt concurred. "You know, I don't know if it's true or not, but I read somewhere that agates don't actually come from the ocean."

Paige nearly gasped out loud. "Agates don't come from the ocean?" she said wanly. *Where did they come from then?* she wondered. In her case, they came from the *Television Shopping Show.* She glanced at Wyatt when he continued speaking.

"I'm no scientist, but I've read that when cliffs along beaches and rivers erode, the agates end up washing out to sea, where they're polished in the surf over time. Ultimately, they end up on the beach, are covered with sand, and when we have storms, the sand is washed away, exposing the agates beneath."

Paige only half listened to Wyatt's explanation. She really felt sick to her stomach now. Finally, she gathered her thoughts and spoke. "Um, is it possible that there's a huge supply of agates somewhere off the coastline that are washing up at Agate Cove, and Mother Nature just hasn't had time to cover them up with sand—you know, sort of skipping over that part?"

Wyatt gave her a curious glance and then shrugged. "That sounds . . . reasonable to me. Hey, you want a sip of coffee?" He passed her a barrel-sized cup of coffee that barely fit in the cup holder. Paige's eyes widened when she spied the huge cup.

"Are you tired?" she asked. "Obviously, you must need caffeine."

"I'm fine. Maybe I am a little tired. But the coffee will perk me right up. Get it—*perk* me right up? Actually, I know how you can perk me up." He leaned in for a kiss.

Paige hadn't expected the kiss, but soon felt herself awash with sensation as his lips pressed against hers with a gentle insistence. He deepened the kiss, until Paige felt as if she were melting against him. He was first to pull back, leaving her feeling slightly disoriented and lost. The kiss, in combination with her shock at seeing the article, caused her to nearly topple over. Wyatt noticed.

"Wow!" he said, a self-satisfied gleam in his eye.

"Wow," Paige echoed softly, and then sank against the seat.

Nobody's kisses had ever caused the kind of reaction in her that Wyatt's had, and for the brief span of time their lips met, she'd forgotten the horror of the article. It had to be significant that he could distract her to that extent. Paige had been in relationships after Wyatt, but none had sparked any kind of real response in her. She felt her face flood with warmth just thinking about Wyatt's kisses. And then she had to wonder, would he still want to kiss her when she was languishing in jail? Because surely that was where she was headed.

She turned to catch him staring at her. "Hey, are you okay? All of a sudden, you don't look so good."

"We should probably get moving," she suggested, attempting a smile.

They backed out of the convenience store and continued along the detour. Wyatt shot worried glances her way. "Paige, you're looking kind of pale," he observed with concern.

"I'm a little carsick," she lied.

"I don't remember you ever getting carsick," he remarked. "Scoot closer. We'll be home soon."

In truth, Paige hated this stretch of road, since if any could induce car sickness, this was it. It felt like a carnival ride, with all the twists and turns and steep inclines. There was also a huge drop-off to her right. Wyatt caught her eyeing the ravine warily. "Hey, don't look at the drop-off. Look over here instead."

Wyatt's handsome face was a far better distraction. He squeezed her tighter against him, and as he had said earlier, it was like they had never been apart—as if their two bodies fit.

Soothed by his closeness, Paige found herself drifting off to sleep. She attempted to stave off slumber, almost embarrassed that she was so tired and that he was forced to do the driving. What the heck was wrong with her?

"I don't know what's wrong with me," she said with a yawn.

"You're tired," he said simply. "Probably all those secrets you and the ladies are keeping are wearing on your conscience."

"I thought we had an agreement," she reminded him, a little too harshly.

He eyed her curiously. "No harm, no foul. Go to sleep, okay?"

Paige continued to fight off sleep, but when Wyatt began gently rubbing her shoulder, she gave up the battle.

When he finally turned onto the sandy lane to Mary's house, it was getting dark and a thick fog had rolled in. They were almost to the house when Paige began thrashing in her sleep. Wyatt quickly shifted the car into park and took her by both shoulders. "Paige, wake up. You're all right. We're home."

Paige was in a dream state still. In her dream, she was on the public beach, about to drop the agates, when she suddenly found herself immersed in quicksand. She fought the sand valiantly. "I need to make the drop," she cried out in her dream.

To Wyatt's surprise, Paige struggled against his imprisoning hands, and then, talking in her sleep, she murmured out loud, "Let go. I have to make the drop."

Wyatt was taken aback for a moment, his eyes widened in shock. *I have to make the drop.*

He sat in stunned surprise for a moment, watching Paige's beautiful face. Still asleep, she was struggling against something. He pulled her against him then, and whispered in her ear, "Wake up. We're home."

Her eyes finally fluttered open. She pulled back, looking disheveled and disoriented. "We're home," she repeated, shaking her head. "I think I had a bad dream." Wyatt nodded, and she saw something in his eyes. "What is it, Wy?"

He attempted to keep his voice neutral when he spoke. "It's nothing. I'd better get these boxes unloaded."

Paige watched him curiously as he climbed out of the truck. Was it her imagination, or did he suddenly look pale?

Mary had heard them drive up and walked out on crutches to greet them. "Where do you want the boxes?" Wyatt asked her.

"The family room is fine," she said, and then glanced at Paige, who had climbed out of the truck. She noticed Paige watching after Wyatt with a worried frown.

Mary also sensed something amiss with Wyatt; he appeared to have the weight of the world on his shoulders. He moved slowly to the back of the truck, his brows knitted together and his mouth set in a grim line.

He carried the boxes into the family room, unwilling to let Paige help him. When he was done, he walked outside. Paige followed. "Are you all right?" she asked him.

"I'm fine."

"Are you coming in?" Paige asked.

"Uh, no, I'd better not. I . . . should go."

Paige watched his retreating figure as he crossed the driveway and climbed the stairs to his apartment. Something was wrong with Wyatt. Something was very wrong.

Chapter Thirteen

Isn't Wyatt coming in?" Mary asked, glancing past Paige to the front door.

"No, I guess not. I . . . don't know why." She shook her head. "He's acting kind of funny all of a sudden."

"We'll worry about Wyatt later," Mary said. "Paige, we have to talk."

"I know what you're going to tell me. I saw the paper," Paige moaned, and then walked into the family room and dropped onto the couch. She tipped her head back and shook it from side to side. "We're going to jail, Gram. Or at least I am, and probably you too. Jeanette and Minnie should get lighter sentences than us, and Dori, well, she'll be all right, since she never did her assigned drops . . ." Paige's eyes widened suspiciously. "Ah, clever Dori, she *knew* what she was doing."

"Paige, sweetheart, you're rambling again. Listen, we have to keep our wits about us. We're not going to jail. Not if I can help it." Mary paused, her eyes passing over Paige's face. "Honey, you don't look so good."

"How do you expect me to look, Gram? And you're right,

121

we're not going to jail—no, it won't be the pokey for us—because we're going to the Big House! We've committed fraud—on an international scale! Pretty soon, those world-renowned scientists will examine those rocks, and you know what they'll say?"

Mary watched her, her eyes widened in dread. She shook her head no.

"They'll say, 'Look, those rocks came from the *Television Shopping Show.*' Gram, the agates are probably fakes!"

Paige's eyes suddenly widened in terror as another dreadful thought occurred to her.

"What is it, Paige?" Mary prompted.

"They're going to figure it out."

"Who is?"

"The folks at the *Television Shopping Show*—they're going to see all this news coverage of those blasted agates, see a picture, and think, 'Wow, those agates look familiar!' *Kabam,* it's the chair for us!"

"Honey, you've taken us from the pokey, to the penitentiary, to the electric chair. I really don't think they're going to fry us for this."

"Ever hear of death by lethal injection?"

"Surely they won't kill us. I'm sure the worst we'll get is life without possibility of parole."

"Gram, by the time this is all said and done, we'll have defrauded hundreds, maybe thousands of people."

"Oh, Paige, how did we defraud them? Sure, we're luring people to the beach under false pretenses, but they leave satisfied. They leave with their agates, happy as clams. They didn't even have to pay for them. I should think they would be grateful." She shook her head, and then scowled and muttered, "Ungrateful tourists."

"Gram, don't make this about them. It's not their fault." Paige ran a hand through her hair. "Oh, this is terrible—*terrible.*"

"Paige, it's going to be okay," Mary said reassuringly, but Paige could see in her eyes that she didn't believe a word she'd said.

Suddenly, Paige's eyes grew as big as saucers as something too terrible to contemplate came to her. Earlier, in the truck, Wyatt had been loving and congenial, but later, he had been somber and uncommunicative. She knew what that meant. She leaped from the couch and began pacing the room. "Oh no, oh no, oh no," she said.

"What is it, Paige?" Mary practically shrieked.

"Wyatt knows! You saw him. His whole manner changed before my eyes. We both saw that article, and later . . . oh, Gram, he's figured it out, and now he's up there in his apartment dealing with the prospect that his girlfriend is a criminal. So much for our future together!"

Mary gasped.

"What is it, Gram?"

"So you and Wyatt were discussing a future together? Oh, that's lovely!"

"Gram, it would have been lovely. Now, it's impossible! The undersheriff can't date a hardened criminal!"

"Paige, you are not hardened. You could never be hardened. You might be between a rock and a hard place, but you are *not* hardened."

Paige glanced up, considered her grandmother's words, and then burst out in nervous laughter. "Gram, did you just make a joke?"

"Not on purpose, I didn't."

Paige dropped back onto the couch. "I really don't feel very well."

Mary grimaced. "You probably don't feel much like making a drop tonight, then. Dori called with some lame excuse about her left knee acting up."

Paige's mouth dropped open. "Gram. Think about what

we've been saying. We can't make the agate drops anymore. It has to stop. Maybe if we stop, everything can go back to normal around here. Maybe all the interest will die down, and we'll get through this unscathed."

"We have to make the drops, at least until the Fourth of July."

"*Why?*" she moaned.

"Paige, we started this to save our town, and we're doing it—saving our town, that is. When Dori called earlier, she mentioned she'd been on her bad knee all day because the souvenir shop was crowded with wall-to-wall customers—all day long, Paige. Minnie called me not long after. Every room at the B and B is booked, and she has a waiting list. The diner is so busy these days that Jeanette can hardly clear out customers fast enough for the people waiting in line."

"You know what, Gram, that's all well and good, but I'm not seeing your fair-weather friends doing their parts to save their own businesses, let alone the town."

"True," she acknowledged. "But Paige, the truth is, we've started this and we may as well finish it. From what I read in the article, the scientists are already analyzing those agates. Samples were sent to them. If there's something to find, they will already have found it. Besides, it's not as if anyone knows it's us distributing the rocks."

"It isn't *us,*" Paige said testily. "It's *me.*"

"Honey, I'd never let you take the fall. I'll confess to the crime if the need arises."

"I'm not letting you go to jail!" Paige shrieked. "You wouldn't last a day in the Big House."

"I'm tougher than I look," Mary assured her.

"Wait a minute, Gram. Why do we have to continue the agate drops through the Fourth of July?"

"Because, apparently, the city council has decided to have a big party on the beach on Independence Day. They're planning a city-wide picnic and fireworks on the sand. It should be fun," she added.

"Nobody told me about this," Paige groaned.

"I just found out today. Martha down at the hall called me."

"Oh, Gram, this just gets worse and worse."

"I see your point," Mary acknowledged. "But regarding the Fourth of July celebration, I was thinking maybe we could drop red, white, and blue agates the night before the party."

"Gram!" Paige shrieked. "*Are you kidding me?*"

Paige woke to the sound of her alarm at 2:30. She attempted to sit up in bed, but her extremities wouldn't cooperate. She felt achy and miserable all over. A hand to her face confirmed she had a fever.

She glanced around her bedroom, and then cocked her head to try to see down the hallway. *Where was Gram?*

She forced herself up and felt unsteady on her feet. "I need Ibuprofen," she moaned. She padded out of the room and into the kitchen, expecting Mary to be there. She wasn't.

Paige found her asleep in her recliner in the family room. She reached out to shake her awake, but thought better of it. Her grandmother had been getting very little sleep over the past weeks, since she had stayed up every minute Paige or the others had been on that beach. Paige decided to let her sleep.

She found the Ibuprofen tablets in the bathroom medicine cabinet, and hurriedly slipped into her shoes and coat. She found the backpack propped against a chair on the kitchen floor. It was already loaded with agates.

Paige hefted it and started off, but remembered the stun gun and pepper spray. She stuffed both items into her coat pocket and then tiptoed down the long hall to the front door. She stepped outside and carefully pulled the door closed behind her.

After casting a furtive glance at Wyatt's apartment, she hunched down and moved as stealthily as she could across the front lawn, and then carefully navigated the sandy trail down to the beach.

Although it was windy tonight, it wasn't as cold as it had been on previous nights. Paige began distributing the agates as quickly as she could manage, but since she was feeling ill, she wasn't moving as quickly as she would have otherwise. When she finally reached the dune, she felt winded, and sat for a moment to rest. She glanced up, noting that a fog was rolling in off the ocean.

Finally, she stood up to make the trek back. As usual, she stayed close to the shoreline, where the waves met the sand. She tramped the agates down as she walked. She realized she should have been paying better attention to the ocean when a sneaker wave struck her and toppled her. To her horror, she found herself in water at least three feet deep. She rose up, sputtering, but the current pulled her feet out from under her, and she felt herself being pulled farther out.

When she rose, she was standing in neck-deep water. She immediately understood the peril she was in, but tried not to panic. She took a deep breath and, with all the strength she could muster, trudged toward the shore, using her hands as rudders. Her teeth chattered mercilessly, and her legs felt so fatigued she wasn't sure she could make it to shore.

Suddenly, she was struck from behind by another large wave, which both knocked her over and propelled her forward. She landed splayed out in the shallow water, and she scurried with the last bit of strength she had onto the dry sand. She fell back panting and with her teeth chattering so forcefully, she thought she might chip a tooth.

She understood how close a call she had just had, realizing she could have easily been swept out to sea. No one would have been the wiser. Even her grandmother would have been unaware that she was missing for several hours, since Paige had left her asleep on the recliner.

Paige realized how careless she had been to leave the house without telling her grandmother. The error in judgment had nearly cost her her life.

She finally rose from the sand and started back home. She'd completely forgotten about the backpack until she spotted it floating in the water. She carefully retrieved it, all the while keeping her eyes on the ocean.

Finally, she trudged back up the hill and to the house. She was cold, stiff, and utterly miserable. At the front door, she tugged off her sopping-wet shoes and then stepped gingerly onto the tiled floor. With her luck tonight, she feared she might slip on the smooth surface.

She headed for the bathroom, where she slipped out of her wet clothes. She turned on the shower, and while waiting for the water to heat up, she caught sight of her reflection in the mirror. Purple half-moons framed her lower lids. Her eyes were watery and red. Her nose felt plugged, and her throat was sore. Every muscle in her body ached.

When she stepped into the shower, she wished she didn't need to wash her hair, but thanks to her submersion into the salty sea, it couldn't be helped. Quickly, she scrubbed her hair and body, her teeth still chattering despite the water's warm temperature. Paige knew she had the flu or a bad cold. It had been coming on before her dip in the ocean.

She sighed ruefully. She suddenly remembered kissing Wyatt in the truck. She felt horrible for possibly infecting him.

After her shower, Paige padded into her bedroom and dressed

in warm pajamas. She towel-dried her hair, combed through it, and then tiptoed in to check on her grandmother. Mary was sleeping soundly on the recliner, her broken foot supported by the leg rest and propped up with pillows.

After assuring herself that Mary was all right, she headed back to the bathroom, where she retrieved another towel. She hated to use another one, but she wrapped her hair in the dry towel, and then lay down in bed.

She fell asleep the instant her head hit the pillow, and when she woke up in the morning, she was hard-pressed to lift her head *off* the pillow.

"I need to see her," Wyatt said firmly. "Please, Mary, it's important."

Mary eyed Wyatt speculatively, attempting to read him. Did he know about the agates, because if so, shouldn't he be yelling at her? She was more culpable than Paige, since Operation Save Agate Cove had been her idea.

"Please, Mary, I need to talk to Paige before I go to work."

Mary shook her head. "I'm sorry, Wyatt. She's not feeling well."

"She's sick?" he asked with concern.

She nodded. "I think it's the flu, or a very bad cold. She's miserable."

"Can you please tell her I need to speak with her?"

Mary shook her head. "Wyatt, she doesn't want you any-where near her. She said something about already exposing you to illness, and that she wasn't going to do it again."

"I'm not worried about getting sick. I never catch anything, anyway."

Mary was adamant. "No, son," she said. She leaned forward and whispered to him, "I don't think she wants you to see her looking so bad."

"I don't care how she looks!" he said, loud enough for Paige to hear. He raked a hand through his hair when he realized how that sounded. "I mean, I do care how she looks—oh, but you know what I mean."

"I do, son. You'd better be going to work now."

For a second, Mary thought he might shoulder his way past her, but she knew he was too gentlemanly to toss an elderly woman aside.

With a beleaguered sigh, he strode toward the door. "I'll be back when my shift is over. Can I see her then?"

Mary shrugged. "It's up to her."

Wyatt left the house and Mary perked her ears. When she heard the patrol car start up, she listened until the sound receded into the wind before she hurried to check on Paige.

"Oh, honey, you do look awful," Mary said. "What hurts?"

"Everything," Paige moaned.

"Oh, Paige, why did you go out there last night? I deliberately didn't set my alarm. After doing some serious thinking, I had decided to forget about last night's drop."

"I'm sorry, Gram," she sniffled. "I didn't realize. But at least it's done."

Paige refrained from mentioning her near-death experience, and Mary left her to rest. She returned moments later, dangling the backpack. She wore a look of alarm on her face.

"Paige, it's wet."

She nodded and said in a raspy voice, "Yeah, I dropped it."

Mary watched her speculatively. "You didn't . . . ?"

"End . . . up . . . in . . . the ocean?" she said from between chattering teeth, just thinking about how cold that ocean water had been.

Mary nodded, appearing to brace for her answer.

"No," Paige said simply.

Mary heaved a sigh of relief. "If I thought you'd been in that ocean, I don't know . . ."

"Gram," she said hoarsely, "it's okay. I'm okay. Hey, did I hear Wyatt out there before?"

Mary nodded. "He wanted to see you. He was awfully insistent. He said he's coming back later."

"Did he . . . have his handcuffs out?" she asked, taking a stab at humor.

Mary couldn't manage a chuckle. "No, honey, he didn't. Now, you need your rest. Sleep, and when you wake up, I'll have homemade chicken soup for you, okay?"

"Sounds . . . good," Paige croaked.

Paige slept until lunchtime, ate a little soup, and then promptly went back to sleep. When she woke up next, it was to the sound of Wyatt's voice demanding to see her again.

She felt groggy and light-headed. She attempted to lift her head, and watched the door briefly. *Had Wyatt come to arrest her?* When he didn't tumble into the room, followed by several law enforcement officers, she fell back against her pillow and went to sleep.

Just outside Paige's bedroom door, Mary blocked his way.

"Mary, you're my friend, and I'm asking you as my friend to let me see Paige. I need to talk to her, and I need to talk to her now."

"Wyatt, it's going to have to wait."

He shook his head. "Don't you understand, Mary? I don't know if it can wait. Paige needs . . . help."

"I'm giving her all the help she needs right now," Mary assured him. "If she needs a doctor, I'll see that she gets one."

"Mary, there are clinics in Portland . . ."

Mary appeared taken aback. "We have doctors much closer than that, Wyatt. You know that."

"The doctors in Portland are the best, and some offer outpatient treatment."

Mary shook her head. *What was Wyatt talking about?*

"Wyatt, I have more soup to make. You're welcome to stop

by later for dinner, but until Paige tells me she's feeling up to visitors, I'm afraid I can't let you see her. You understand, don't you?"

"Oh, I understand all right," he said angrily.

He stormed off, and Mary couldn't quite make out what he was saying as he grumbled all the way to the door. Was it something about her being an . . . enabler . . . ? No, that couldn't possibly be it.

Chapter Fourteen

Paige was ill with a bad cold that hung on for more than a week. Unfortunately, just as she thought she was getting better, she had developed an ear infection. She woke in the night with ear pain so intense, Mary had called the local doctor, a good friend, who agreed to make a house call. He prescribed antibiotics and pain meds, and by the third day of treatment, she was feeling well enough to rejoin the human race.

Mary noticed she was finally looking better as the two sat down to breakfast one morning. "You had me worried, honey," she said. "I wasn't sure you were ever going to get well."

"I wasn't sure I was going to get well either," she acknowledged. "When I get a cold, I usually end up with an ear infection, which inevitably turns into a sinus infection."

"You'd better stay in until we're absolutely certain you're well."

"You know, I'm still shocked to hear that the ladies picked

up my agate-distributing duties while I was down for the count. How did you convince them to finally do their parts?" Paige asked.

Mary held a piece of toast poised in front of her mouth. "I threatened them," she said matter-of-factly, and then took a bite.

"You did what?"

"I told them if they didn't step up to the plate and do their parts, I was going to go to Wyatt and spill the beans. I told them you were at death's door, thanks to your service to this town, and that they should be ashamed of themselves for placing the whole burden on you."

"Huh—well, it apparently worked."

"Yes, and they were particularly compliant when I told them I was going to tell Wyatt the whole scheme was Dori's idea."

"And they bought it—really?"

She nodded. "They knew Dori would sing like a bird. She's as weak-kneed as her weak knee."

Paige nodded in measured intervals. "Huh—well, at least we'll all go down together. Maybe they'll give us adjoining cells at the state pen."

Mary considered Paige's words. "I'd bet so. Wyatt probably has friends in high places. He's such a good-natured person— well, most of the time anyway—and people seem to respond to him."

"True," Paige mused. "I'd like to think he'll use whatever pull he has on our behalves."

"Uh, Paige," Mary began tentatively, "are you ready to see Wyatt yet? I think you should. I've been thinking, if he knew about Operation Save Agate Cove, and our early-morning agate drops, well, wouldn't he have thrown the book at us by now?"

"I've been thinking about that myself. If he knew, why

didn't he question you? It only makes sense. Gram, it gets curiouser and curiouser."

"And we get luckier and luckier," Mary observed. "How the heck did those agates fool those supposed world-renowned scientists?"

"I guess a rock is a rock is a rock," Paige said.

"Lucky for us," Mary reiterated.

"So, does this mean that Operation Save Agate Cove will still end on the Fourth of July?"

Mary sighed. "After that close call we had, I just don't know. Do we continue to push our luck? I do know that, with the girls helping out, the scheme is going much more smoothly. Maybe we *can* pull it off—see it to its natural conclusion. What do you think?"

Paige considered the question. "I don't know. I guess I'll have a better idea about what to do when I actually come face-to-face with Wyatt again. I need to see with my own two eyes that he doesn't know about the agates, and then I'll feel better about everything." She shook her head. "That day we drove to Portland, everything was great, but by the time we got home, *something* had changed. I need to know what."

She continued, "If he does know about those agates, then we've put *him* between a rock and a hard place. It won't be easy for him, having to arrest me."

"Maybe he won't arrest you—us. Maybe he'll understand that everything we've done, we've done for the good of the town." Mary paused, her expression thoughtful for a moment. "Let's just hope we get a sympathetic jury."

"Gram, do you think we'll end up going to trial?"

"You never know." Mary made a pitiful, disheartened face that made Paige want to bawl, until her grandmother said, "Okay, how did you like that one? Or maybe this one is better . . ." Mary proceeded to demonstrate a series of hang-dog facial expressions for Paige's benefit, finally settling on one. "Is this one most convincing, do you think? I think it says 'I'm a well-intentioned elderly woman who simply made a poor choice, but whose heart was in the right place.' Oh, I know!" Mary said brightly, "I'll also want to hang on to my crutches, you know, kind of hobble into the court room. What do you think, Paige?"

Paige shook her head bemusedly. "I think I don't really know you."

"Oh, you do too. We're two peas in a pod. And this pea doesn't want to do time in a jail pod."

Paige laughed. "Gram, did you just make another joke?"

"If I did, I didn't mean to."

Paige sighed. "I'm worried about Wyatt. He could ultimately be the one most hurt by this. Once again, I've made a choice that has serious implications for him."

"You still love him, don't you?"

Paige couldn't deny it.

"Honey, do you think you should have talked to him any one of the thirty or so times he stopped by to see you while you were sick?"

Paige's expression was pained when she answered. "I don't know . . . Okay, yeah, I probably should have. Do you know if he's home?"

Mary gave a sad smile. "Honey, he's gone to Lincoln City for the week. He stopped by last night and said something about having business to attend to."

"What time was that, Gram?"

"It was late, well after you went to bed. I was stretched out in my recliner, watching television, when he came by."

Paige felt a vague sense of disappointment and abandonment. Up until today, she'd at least had the knowledge that he was close by, should she want to see him. Now that she did, he was a hundred-mile-plus detour away.

"Gram, did he say if he'd be back by the Fourth?"

"No, hon, he didn't."

The Fourth of July marked both America's independence and Mary's first day of independence from her cast. She was positively gleeful.

"I'm looking forward to this picnic," she told Paige eagerly. "I wish I didn't have to use these crutches, however."

"Hey, count your blessings," Paige said. "The doctor said your foot has healed perfectly." Paige stuffed a couple bottles of water into her beach bag. "You know, Gram, I could have driven us to the beach. Why is Dori's grandson picking us up, again?"

"Dori said parking is going to be at a premium in Agate Cove unless we got there at four in the morning, and I didn't want to get there that early. She doesn't have to worry about parking, since she cordoned off a few of the parking spaces at the souvenir shop."

"And which of Dori's grandsons is driving us?"

"He's the only grandson she has."

"He's the dud, right? Why is it again that he's a dud?"

"Well, personally, I think it's because he's nineteen and has yet to hear the word 'no.' Those parents of his dote on that kid. Dori too. It'll be a wonder if he ever manages to be self-supporting."

"Well, maybe he'll surprise them."

"I hope so."

"Is the dud a safe driver? What's his name? I'm afraid if I keep referring to him as 'the dud,' I'll slip up and call him a dud to his face."

Mary shrugged. "I'm sure he's heard it before."

"Gram!" Paige exclaimed.

Mary attempted to look repentant, but it was short-lived. "If memory serves, I think his name is Lester. But, in fairness to the dud, if you saddle a kid with that moniker, you get what you get."

"You are a dud! And a letch!"

After extracting Lester's hand from her knee for the hundredth time, Paige turned to him with blazing eyes. "Do you not understand English? If you don't stop grabbing my knee, I *will* tell your grandmother."

Paige glanced around the beach. Hundreds of blankets were spread out over the sand, with people of all ages enjoying the holiday. The parking lot adjacent to the public beach was also teeming with people, many waiting in lines at assorted food booths for hot dogs and pizza. Even Jeanette had set up a booth, with her staff serving up hamburgers to hungry customers.

Paige started when Lester boldly laid his hand on her knee once again. Did he think she wouldn't notice the gesture? She turned on him with angry eyes. "That's *it!*" she cried.

She rose from the sand and searched for her grandmother. She spied her sitting in a lawn chair at the perimeter of the parking lot, facing the ocean. Her crutches made walking the sandy beach too difficult.

Paige noticed that Dori and Minnie sat on either side of her grandmother. The threesome appeared to be a happy group, despite Mary's recent heavy-handed tactics to convince them to do their parts for Operation Save Agate Cove. Paige had to admit, after seeing all the happy tourists currently at Agate Cove, the future looked bright for the town.

Suddenly, Paige felt a hand hovering precariously close to her thigh. She slapped it away. Usually not one for histrionics, she felt like screaming right now. She took a deep, steadying breath. "Lester!"

How had she gotten stuck sharing a blanket with this college-aged Casanova? He had orchestrated it, that's how.

"You're a feisty one," Lester said, unperturbed, his upturned eyes bright with hopeful anticipation. "I like 'em feisty."

"Oh, good grief!" Paige muttered as she stormed off in the direction of her grandmother. Mary watched her with concern as Paige bent to speak in her ear. "I'm going for a walk. I won't be long."

"Is it the dud?" Mary whispered.

Paige nodded, and Mary nodded knowingly in return. "Are your stun gun and pepper spray in your pocket?"

Paige bit back a chuckle, but to her surprise, when she made a play of patting her pockets, she found an item in either pocket. She realized she must have forgotten to take them out when she'd last worn the coat, on one of her agate-dropping mornings.

"Paige," Dori said with a wink, "I think Lester is just a little bit sweet on you."

Paige bit back a retort. She was decidedly sour on *him*.

"He's going to make some girl a fine husband someday . . ." Dori added in a singsong voice.

Paige forced a smile. "I . . . , don't . . . think . . . so," she muttered under her breath, as she headed to check out Agate Cove's version of a Fourth of July farmer's market. Several booths were set up on Main Street, selling everything from taffy to fine jewelry. Paige noticed with chagrin that one booth was even selling baggies of the agates she and the ladies had dropped onto the beach.

As she strolled along, taking in the sights and sounds of the bustling town, she wondered where Wyatt might be. Was he still in Lincoln City tending to police business? She hadn't heard from him. Her heart twisted at the thought that he might have given up on her.

If only she had allowed him to visit her when she was ill. But then, she had feared he knew her secret, and she hadn't been able to face him. Later, as she realized he probably wasn't on to her and the ladies, she felt an urgent need to keep it that way. If they could just keep tourists coming to Agate Cove until the roads opened, she and Wyatt could focus on their future after.

She told herself she was protecting him—both from catching her cold and from the possible repercussions of Operation Save Agate Cove. She knew that she and the ladies weren't out of the woods yet.

Paige left Main Street and crossed the road to the parking lot where the food vendors were set up. She wasn't particularly hungry yet, but she strolled along anyway, for something to do. She had no intention of rejoining Lester on his beach blanket.

For a brief second, she contemplated going to her car to retrieve a blanket she had stowed in the trunk, but then she remembered she didn't have her car. The dud had driven her and Mary.

As if on cue, Lester appeared, grinning broadly and invading her personal space. Once again, he was too close for comfort. "Where'd you go?" he asked.

"I went for a walk," she told him in measured tones. "And . . . I think I'll grab a bite to eat. Will you excuse me, Lester?"

"I'll join you," he said gamely.

"No, Lester, you will not."

She saw a flash of disappointment in his eyes, but it was soon replaced by his ridiculous brand of bravado. "Ah, you know you want me with you today. I can see it in your eyes."

"What you're seeing in my eyes, Lester, is frustration and contempt. Now, I don't want to be mean to you, but if I have to, I will. And . . . as I said before, I'm not above talking to your grandmother."

"She'd never believe a negative word about me," he said smoothly.

"Shall we find out?"

He appeared to weigh her threat, and then grinned wickedly. "I'm prepared to take my chances."

When the boy snaked a hand out and laced his fingers through her hair and pulled her face toward him, she was so shocked by the gesture, she didn't even register that he intended to kiss her. When his lips met hers, she gasped, and he took the reflexive action as an invitation and pulled her even closer.

She struggled against his imprisoning arms, mortified by his actions, and more mortified by the number of people who possibly had a front row seat to his amorous attentions toward her. Her face flamed, and with superhuman strength, she shoved him away. She wiped at her mouth with a shaky hand, and then aimed a finger at his face. "You are a creep!"

When the persistent boy took a step closer to her, still smiling that same cocky smile, she instinctively reached for the pepper spray in one pocket of her coat and the stun gun in the other. She eyed each in her hands for a second, and then opted for the stun gun. Although she didn't really intend to use it on him, he wouldn't know that.

"If you make another move toward me, I'm going to zap you and then watch you flop around on the concrete like a fish out of water," she threatened.

"You wouldn't," Lester said with a confident chuckle, "not with all these people around."

"Try me."

Lester cocked his head to the side and took a quick step toward her. Paige instinctively raised the stun gun in a flash, when a large, firm hand clasped her hand and gently extracted the gun from it. In her hyper-sensitive state, she nearly deployed the pepper spray, but that too was taken from her before she could register what was happening. She turned around, ready to duke it out with whomever was behind her, when she spied Wyatt's stern face.

"It's all right, Paige. I'll deal with him," he said in a soothing but firm tone.

Lester registered immediately by the look on Wyatt's face that he had crossed the line. He raised both hands and began backing off. "Hey, no big deal," he said, a high-pitched tone to his voice.

Wyatt aimed a finger at him. "Don't move!"

He turned to Paige. "Are you all right?"

She nodded, and then glared at the boy.

Wyatt took a step closer to Lester and stared menacingly into his face. "Hear me, and hear me good. *'No' means no.* If I ever see you near Paige again, or if I see you do anything to any woman in this town, you and I are going to have plenty of time getting to know one another, since you'll be in the back of my patrol car and taking a very long detour to Lincoln City. Do we understand each other?"

Lester nodded his head and backed away before spinning on his heel and running off. "I will be having a talk with your father!" Wyatt called after him.

"And I'm going to have a talk with your grandmother!" Paige added for good measure.

Wyatt turned his attention to Paige, who was visibly shaken by the encounter. "Are you all right?" he asked, his eyes passing over her face.

She nodded. "He's a stupid, stupid kid—the arrogance of him practically attacking me in such a public setting!"

The color drained from Wyatt's face. "Thank God he didn't try anything in an isolated setting. Paige, stay away from that kid. I will be keeping an eye on him."

"You don't have to tell me twice."

Wyatt nodded and then glanced around. He also seemed shaken, and Paige suspected he was taking a moment to gather his thoughts. "Big crowd," he said finally, and she realized he was attempting to make small talk. "You're looking better."

He appeared to scrutinize every inch of her face, his brows furrowed. "Mary said you've been really sick."

She nodded. "I caught a bad cold, which turned into a horrible ear infection. I, uh, know you stopped by to see me, but I didn't want to risk infecting you."

He looked skeptical, and she wasn't sure what to make of it.

"But you're feeling better now." It was a statement, not a question.

"I'm still on antibiotics, but I'm on the mend."

He nodded distractedly. "I was about to get something to eat when I saw the little punk harassing you. Would you care to join me?"

Paige glanced out over the crowd, suddenly wishing she was home and away from the bustling tourists. She'd also realized earlier that although the beach wasn't as windy as it often was, it was gusty enough, and the last thing she needed was to be outside when she was still fighting an ear infection.

"Well?" he prompted.

"Oh, sorry—I was just thinking it would be nice to get away from this place." The instant she said the words, she realized it sounded like an invitation. "Oh, I didn't mean . . ."

"Then let's get out of here," he said.

"But what about Gram? Lester drove us this morning."

"I'll go talk to her. I'll be right back."

"Are you sure, Wy?"

"Yeah. No worries."

No worries. If only that were true.

Chapter Fifteen

Sitting in the front seat of Wyatt's patrol car, Paige cast a worried glance at the backseat. She was surprised to see the seats were a hard plastic and looked terribly uncomfortable. There were no door handles back there either, which made her shudder. She had a tendency to get claustrophobic and suspected that the long ride to jail in the back of the patrol car would be a miserable experience—exacerbated by the one-hundred-mile-plus detour. And once she got to jail, how would she ever adapt to a tiny cell?

By the time Wyatt rounded the front of the car and climbed into the driver's seat, Paige wore a sickly expression on her face.

"Are you all right?" he asked.

She nodded. "Was Gram okay with me leaving the picnic early?"

"She was fine. I told her I'd pick her up later. She seemed downright pleased to see the two of us talking." He raked a hand through his hair. "Frankly, that confounds me, because she sure wouldn't let me anywhere near you when you were 'sick.'"

Why had Wyatt put an emphasis on the word 'sick'? Paige wondered. Perhaps she had heard him wrong.

"To be honest, Wy, I didn't want you to see me looking so horrible." *That, and other things,* she thought grimly, and nearly groaned out loud.

"I don't know why you're so worried about what you look like when you're sick."

"It's a woman thing, I guess. Wyatt, my eyes were puffy, my nose was red, and I was burning up with a *contagious* fever. I'm actually surprised you didn't catch it anyway."

"You mean, since we kissed on the drive home from Portland? Yeah, *funny* I didn't catch anything."

Paige wasn't sure what he meant by that. Hadn't she heard him say he never caught colds—which she knew was an exaggeration anyway—but then, why would he think it was funny he hadn't caught her cold? Besides, maybe she hadn't actually been contagious at that point. She tried to recall. *Had her fever set in yet?*

She shook her head to clear it. Why was she worried about inconsequential details? She had bigger fish to fry, but . . . she didn't really want to think about that either. She took a stab at making small talk instead. "I understand you've been working in Lincoln City."

"Yep, that's true."

"So you've been busy?"

"Yep, I have."

Paige tipped her head to the side and eyed him curiously. Why was he giving short answers to her questions all of a sudden?

"Is something wrong, Wyatt?" Suddenly, her eyes widened. Wyatt was behaving so oddly. Maybe he did know about the agates. Paige leaned back against the seat, and then cast another worried glance at the hard plastic in the back. Soon, she would know just how hard that plastic was . . .

When Wyatt didn't answer her question, Paige turned in the seat and stared out at the ocean. It was so beautiful, she mused.

Finally, Wyatt broke the silence. "That was quite a party going on in town. Those agates have brought tourists here in numbers," he observed.

Paige practically jumped out of her seat. She took a deep breath before turning to him. She tried to read his face, but he continued to stare straight ahead at the road. Was that muscle in his jaw clenching? She couldn't tell, and leaned slightly closer for a look.

He turned at that instant and gave her a bewildered glance. She pulled back quickly and turned back to the window and the ocean view.

"Those agates really saved this town," Wyatt said.

Paige gulped.

"I understand that the scientists don't have a clue why the agates have started washing up in such numbers, but they still think it's some sort of unusual natural phenomenon."

"Could be," Paige mused, without glancing his way.

"Of course, all the attention on the town and the influx of tourists brings a whole new set of problems."

"Really?" Paige said, still failing to look at him.

"Oh, yeah, you know, with Agate Cove's Main Street being so narrow, there's always the fender bender happening, or a car prowl by some kid. And there are always the rowdy high schoolers and college kids making noise."

"Yes, I see what you mean," Paige said, still refraining from looking at him.

"Paige, is there a reason you're looking away from me when I'm talking to you?" Wyatt asked with interest.

Yeah, because you're clearly on to me. But she didn't say the words. Instead, she turned to face him and smiled brightly. "Oh, there's no reason—sorry."

Wyatt turned to meet her gaze, his eyes narrowed. "So Paige, what were you doing carrying a stun gun and pepper spray in your coat pocket?"

Paige stiffened. "What stun gun and pepper spray?" She pressed her eyelids shut and nearly groaned aloud. *Had she really just said that?*

Wyatt actually chuckled. "*What* boxes, and *what* stun gun and pepper spray? Paige, what is going on with you? God knows I wish you'd tell me."

"Nothing!" she said. *Hey,* she thought. *He doesn't know. He really doesn't know.* "I . . . didn't even know I had a stun gun and pepper spray in my pocket," she told him. "Gram pulled the coat out of the closet and passed it to me. I discovered them later, and if you hadn't shown up, they might have come in very handy." *Sorry Gram,* she thought. *It's every girl for herself right now.*

"Why would Mary give you a stun gun and pepper spray?" Wyatt mused aloud, stroking his jaw. "Does she know more about this Lester kid than we do? Maybe I need to have a word with her."

"Oh, the kid's probably harmless," Paige said quickly. "I could have taken him down."

"With or without the stun gun and pepper spray?"

"Oh, I was getting motivated pretty fast," she said. "The little punk—I probably could have dropped him with a palm to his nose and a knee to his . . . well, you get the drift."

Wyatt suddenly looked angry. "If he ever bothers you again, you'll tell me . . . ?"

She nodded and then smiled, attempting to lighten the mood. "Thanks for coming in time to save him, by the way. If I'd actually zapped the little weasel, it might have done irreparable harm to Gram's and Dori's friendship."

"Not to mention the harm it might have done to the little weasel. Would you really have used the stun gun on him?"

"No," Paige conceded. "I just wanted to scare him."

Wyatt surprised her when he reached across the seat and took her hand. He gave it a gentle squeeze. When he sighed wearily, she wasn't sure what to make of it.

"Wyatt, are you all right?"

"I'm . . . worried about . . . you," he said.

"Wyatt, please don't."

He turned to her with earnest eyes. "You asked me to trust you, but I'm going to ask you to trust me. You need to confide in me, Paige. Something is going on with you. I think I know what it might be, but I'd like you to trust me enough to tell me yourself."

"Wyatt, I thought we had an understanding." She searched his face. "I thought . . . you were willing to give me time."

"Time isn't going to solve your problem, sweetheart. Frankly, I think time is of the essence." He sighed and squeezed her hand again. "Look, I'm hungry. Let's grab something to eat, and then if you're ready to talk, and I hope you are, we'll . . . talk."

Paige made a bewildered face. What the heck was he talking about?

Suddenly, a car whizzed past them, obviously well in excess of the speed limit. Wyatt sighed. "I really should go after that car and ticket the driver . . ."

He appeared to be weighing his next move. "What the heck, I'll probably catch him on the rebound. It's not as if getting out of here is easy. Of course, his having made the detour is probably punishment enough. It doesn't seem fair, really, rewarding the brave soul willing to make the detour with a citation. Besides, with you in the car, I have to think about your safety, and I'm not about to drop you off on the side of the road . . ."

Paige noted that Wyatt was rambling on like she did when

she was a nervous wreck. "Wyatt, are you okay?" she asked. "Now you have me worried."

He waved off her concern. "I'm all right. It's you we have to think about right now," he said sincerely.

Once again, she cast him a quizzical glance. The poor man appeared tortured. Why was that? If he wasn't privy to her clandestine agate-dropping ventures, then what?

He glanced in the rearview mirror, apparently still preoccupied by the speeding motorist. "Those tourists keep the town alive, but sometimes I'm not sure it's worth all the trouble. During the summer, this stretch of road is like a raceway."

Paige only nodded, still watching his profile very carefully.

"If it's not speeding tourists, it's something else," he muttered.

Paige acknowledged his words with a nod, and he continued. "I guess a couple of weeks ago, Deputy Harada was checking out the parking lot at the public beach, since a couple of cars were parked there after-hours. Anyway, he happened to glance out at the ocean and saw a sneaker wave catch some woman. Why she was on that beach in the middle of the night . . . ?"

Paige gasped.

"I know," Wyatt said softly. "It's awful. Anyway, Harada said the wave took her out. He said he ran toward the beach, pulling off his shoes as he went, but stopped to call dispatch to alert rescue personnel. Apparently in the time he stopped and glanced down and then back up, he lost sight of her. A fog had rolled in. So . . . now, we have to wonder, was she swept out to sea? I'm afraid it's highly likely."

He shook his head with a long sigh. "We've been checking missing persons reports, but so far nothing has turned up." He turned and snared her gaze. "Why would some woman risk her life like that, walking so close to the waves late at night, disregarding the postings that the beach is closed from dusk to six A.M.? Had to be a tourist," he muttered. "A townie wouldn't have been so reckless. Either way, I feel sick about it."

Paige gulped loudly, and then felt her throat tightening. She felt sick about it too. She managed a shaky nod. "Must have been a tourist," she agreed, attempting to keep her voice steady. "But who knows? Maybe the woman made it back to shore."

"It's not likely. If she panicked—" Wyatt shook his head. "I doubt I could have made it out if I were in her position," he acknowledged.

Paige sat frozen in the seat. So a deputy had seen her that night on the beach. What if he had managed to catch up to her? If he had, she'd already know how hard the plastic seats in the back of the patrol car felt after a very long drive.

Wyatt pulled off the road and into a pizza establishment that sat alone on a knoll overlooking the ocean. He turned off the ignition. "Does pizza sound all right to you? I can run inside and grab one, and we can take it back to your place."

"That's fine," Paige said, "but are you allowed to do this while on duty?"

"I'm entitled to a lunch hour," he said with a laugh. "Are you worried about your tax dollars being wasted by a lackadaisical cop? Because the truth is, I work around-the-clock these days. With the North and South holes to deal with, and then all the issues with tourists I mentioned to you, I hardly know if I'm coming or going anymore."

"I know you work hard, Wyatt, but I mean, well, you have a civilian in your car with you. Is *that* a problem?"

"No, but if someone wants to make it a problem, let 'em. Besides, I'm escorting you home after an encounter with a guy who might very well be a predator."

"I think he's just a stupid college kid."

"I hope you're right. Okay, what sounds good to you?"

"Anything's good."

"I'll be right back."

While she waited for Wyatt to return, she revisited their earlier conversation. She couldn't make sense of any of it. Relief flooded through her that Wyatt apparently didn't know about her efforts related to Operation Save Agate Cove, but clearly he had been trying to convey to her that he knew *something.*

Suddenly, she had a splitting headache, and her ear began to throb. She noted again that she probably should have stayed out of the wind today, since her still-sensitive ear was so prone to infection.

When Wyatt returned to the car, carrying the pizza, he passed it to her. "Careful, it's hot."

She positioned the steaming pizza on her lap so as to keep from being burned, and then stared out the window at the ocean. Sometimes she imagined all the mysteries and secrets in the depths of that ocean. Unfortunately, she was fast beginning to realize that mysteries and secrets weren't all they were cracked up to be.

Back at Paige's grandmother's house, Wyatt followed her inside. He dropped the pizza box onto the kitchen table.

"Excuse me a minute," Paige said, and then dashed to her bedroom to grab a pain pill from the medicine bottle beside her bed. Her ear was killing her now, and she hoped the infection wasn't flaring up again. She couldn't manage to get the top off the bottle, and finally, in frustration, carried it to Wyatt. "Would you mind opening this?" she asked him.

"What is it?" he asked, staring intently at the label. Paige had picked at the label one day while lying in bed, sick and fighting boredom, and Wyatt couldn't decipher the name of the medication. "Are you sure you need this, Paige? Really sure?"

"It's my pain pill," she said, watching him curiously, "for my ear infection."

He only cocked his head and stared at her. When he made no move to open the medicine bottle, she took it from him and tried to open it herself, to no avail. She thrust it at him. "Will you please open this? My ear really hurts."

With a resigned sigh, Wyatt opened the bottle. She reached to take it from him, but he held it away from her grasp, and proceeded to tip one pill into his hand. He studied it briefly in the palm of his hand before passing it to her. She took it, watching him through narrowed eyes. Why was he so darned interested in that pill?

"Do you have a headache, Wyatt?" she asked him. "If so, I can't offer you one of my pills, but I'd be glad to get you an aspirin."

Wyatt shook his head sadly and capped the medicine bottle tightly. "I don't want any pill. Pills aren't the answer."

"The answer to *what?* I do tend to think they're the answer to my earache—that, and staying out of the wind."

When he took her by the shoulders and stared intently into her eyes, she thought he might be about to kiss her, but instead he held her away from him and shook his head. His eyes fell on the pizza, fast getting cold on the table. "Let's eat, and then we'll talk," he said finally.

When Wyatt suggested they picnic down on her grand-mother's private beach, Paige watched him quizzically. "It's a little bit windy down there," she pointed out.

"What's a little wind?" he said. "The truth is, Paige, that little cove is meaningful to both of us—it's where we fell in love the first time. I'd like to talk to you there, if you're okay with that."

"Well, I'm okay with it, but I can't really speak for my ear . . ."

Paige retrieved a blanket from the family room and followed Wyatt out the front door. He carried the pizza, while
she carried a couple of sodas. He balanced the pizza box and
held her hand until they reached the sandy beach below.

He passed her the pizza and took the blanket. He snapped it
out and spread it on the sand, and then put the box down and
opened it. "Pizza looks good," he said somberly.

"Yeah, the pizza looks good," she said, watching him as if
he were a space alien.

Together, they sat on the blanket, facing the ocean. The
waves lapped the shore, calmer here than they had been on the
public beach earlier. Although the wind wasn't horribly gusty,
it was breezy enough to be a concern. Paige attempted to keep
the wind out of her ear by turning just so.

The couple ate in silence, until Wyatt pointed off toward the
wet shoreline several yards away. "Huh," he said. "Look at that.
There aren't any agates over here. Does that seem odd to you?"

Paige felt as if she'd been punched in the stomach. *He
knew.* Wyatt knew everything. She turned toward him as if
pulled by an invisible string she couldn't break. She expected
to see accusations in his eyes, but he looked . . . perplexed.

Paige took it as her cue. She'd proven herself to be a lousy
liar. Maybe if she put some distance between the two of them,
she could manage to get through this unscathed.

She rose and began walking the shoreline, her head bent to
study it, but with one hand covering her bad ear. She dropped
down to the sand at one point, glanced around her and found a
small stick, and then made a play of digging into the wet sand.
Finally, she rose up, glanced around as if she were puzzling
out a mystery, and then returned to Wyatt and sat down.

"No agates," she said, careful to avoid his gaze as she picked
up her pizza slice.

"Must be some natural phenomenon to account for the

agates on that side of the rise, versus this side," Wyatt observed.

"Maybe it has something to do with the big sand dune that cuts across the public beach," Paige said.

"Who knows?" Wyatt mused. "Are you done eating? We'll have to put the leftovers in the fridge, but first, let's . . . talk."

"Okay," Paige said, situating herself on the blanket to assure her ear stayed as much out of the wind as possible, which was proving pretty impossible. Finally, she simply reached up and covered her ear with her hand.

"Don't you want to hear what I have to say?" Wyatt asked obtusely.

"Sure, but I'd also like to keep my hearing well into my golden years," Paige said, eyeing him curiously.

"Okay, Paige, let's cut the charade."

"What charade?"

"Paige, just . . . talk to me, please. I want to help you. Please know that nothing you tell me is going to make me stop loving you."

"Okay, that's good to know."

Actually, it *was* kind of good to know that, considering there was a real possibility she might do jail time in the near future. Could their love survive her incarceration? In her mind's eye, she envisioned Wyatt bringing her a cake with a file inside. Nope, it wouldn't happen. The image evaporated with a *poof*.

Wyatt watched her curiously. "Paige, where did you go just then? You were obviously light years away."

"Oh, uh, sorry—what were you saying?" She distractedly dropped her hand off her ear. When she felt a big gust of wind swoosh into it, she raised a hand to it again, to block any additional gusty assaults to the now painful, throbbing ear.

"Are you cold?"

"A little," she admitted. "And my ear is killing me. We should really get back up to Gram's."

Had Wyatt just given her a skeptical look?

To Paige's surprise, he reached out to pull her toward him. He situated her with her back to him and wrapped her in his arms. "Better?" he asked.

"Yes," she said and snuggled against him, "except for my ear . . ."

He was silent for a moment. When he kissed the side of her cheek, she turned toward him to meet his lips, but then thought better of it. She wasn't well yet. Although the doctor said she wasn't contagious courtesy of the antibiotics, she wouldn't take a chance with Wyatt's health. She turned her face to the ocean once again.

"You won't kiss me?" he asked, sounding a little hurt.

"I might still be a walking germ. My ear is really bothering me. I'd rather not take any chances with your health. Can you imagine the state of disarray Agate Cove would fall in without you there to keep order?"

He didn't respond, only reached forward, and to her puzzlement, pushed up the left sleeve on her jacket. She turned to see his face. "What are you doing?"

"Nothing." He stroked her arm with his warm hand, but appeared to be looking for something at the same time. When he reached for her other arm and tried to push back the sleeve, she spun away from him and watched him curiously.

"Wyatt, what are you doing? I think it's time for *you* to do some talking."

"Okay, yeah, fine," he said, punctuating each word. "I'll do some talking. I'll gladly start first, since you obviously don't trust me enough to open up to me."

"Okay, good then, go on . . ." She knew her voice had an edge to it, but it couldn't be helped. "Why don't *you* open up to *me,* Wyatt?"

Paige moved away from him and sat back in the sand to watch his face, absently reaching up to cover her infected ear with her hand. Wyatt had turned toward the ocean briefly, and when he turned back, his striking blue eyes filled with apprehension.

"Wyatt, talk!"

"Okay, look, I know something is going on with you, and I think you're in over your head. I want you to know I can help you with that. I have friends."

"Friends?"

"Lawyers," he said succinctly.

Good to know, she thought, *but what is he talking about? Oh, no—does he know about Operation Save Agate Cove?*

"But first, we'll get you some help," Wyatt said softly, interrupting her thoughts.

Paige shook her head. "Help . . . with what?"

He raked a hand through his sandy blond hair. "Look, in my truck on the way home from Portland, you said something—something in your sleep, something that . . . alarmed me."

Okay, we're getting somewhere, she thought. *This has to explain his changed manner toward me that night.*

"I was talking in my sleep?" she said. *Oh, geez, wait, this can't be good.* "What'd I say?" she ventured, preparing for his answer.

"First, Paige, tell me, what was in those boxes we picked up, and the boxes at Mary's house?"

"You said you would trust me about that, Wyatt," she reminded him.

"You do know what's in them, then?" he asked.

"Okay, yes, I do. But Wy, I can't tell you. Eventually, maybe—oh, I don't know—maybe not—but please, Wy, I'm not telling you for your own good. I can't risk . . ."

"You can't risk what?" He watched her fearfully.

"You're a law enforcement officer. I would never want to put you in a perilous situation where your job is concerned."

"Okay, you're really scaring me now."

"*Wyatt,* what did I say in my sleep?"

He emitted a haggard sigh. "You said . . . , 'I have to make the drop.' "

Paige groaned. *That was just great.* So she had been dreaming about dropping those agates on the beach. If memory served, upon waking from it, the dream was actually more like a nightmare. That made sense, since Operation Save Agate Cove had itself come to feel like a nightmare.

Wyatt watched the emotions crisscross her face. His gut told him she had a secret—a big one. And he was terrified.

Paige attempted to sound nonchalant when she spoke again. "So what, Wy? I was dreaming. People say funny things in their sleep all the time."

"Give me some credit, Paige. I know what it meant."

"You do? What did it mean, Wyatt?"

He pinned her with a look.

Her eyes widened as understanding dawned like a mallet upside her head. She leaped to her feet. The implications of his words came crashing down on her. She remembered all his cryptic remarks in the car on the way over, and just now, he was checking her arms for . . . Oh, she knew what he was checking her arms for.

"Wyatt Hall, if that isn't the stupidest thing I've ever heard!"

She began pacing the sand, storming around in erratic circles, and then stopped only long enough to kick sand at him.

He rose and took a step toward her. "Now, Paige, calm down. I want to help you."

"You think . . . ? *You* think . . . ? *You think . . . ?* Oh, Wyatt, how could you *possibly think . . . ?*" She jammed an angry finger his way. "I know it's been ten years since we've spent time together, but you should know me better than *that.*"

She stormed around the sand for a moment, muttering under her breath, her hand clasped over her throbbing ear. She finally stopped and glared at him. "All that talk about picking up where we left off, about everything being the same—*right.*"

She began stomping around in the sand again. If she *had* found any agates on the wet sand earlier, she would have picked them up and begun throwing them at him.

"Paige, calm down. Let me help you."

"Wyatt Hall! You're telling me . . ." She shook her head as if the words were too ridiculous to voice. "You're telling me you suspect me of . . ." She spoke in a low whisper. "You think I'm . . . using drugs?"

Suddenly, her eyes became as big as saucers. "Wait, no, that's not all, is it? *You think I'm a drug trafficker!?*"

Wyatt glanced around, afraid someone might have heard her. "Paige, please, calm down. We sure don't want anyone to hear us. We have to talk about this—quietly."

"Wyatt Hall, I'm not sure I'll ever talk to you again." Suddenly she felt a stabbing pain in her ear. She moaned loudly. "Great—just great—my ear is worse, and for *this!*"

Wyatt took a step toward her, his hand extended in a gesture intended to calm her. It didn't work. She shrank from him, and his accusations. Her eyes filled with tears. "Don't you even think about touching me, Wyatt Hall—ever . . . again!"

Chapter Sixteen

Is the hot water bottle helping?" Mary asked.

"A little," Paige said. She was lying in bed, fighting a fever, and hoping the higher-powered antibiotics the doctor had prescribed the day before might finally end this incessant ear infection.

"The doctor said you should be feeling much better by tomorrow," Mary said sympathetically. "Do you need anything, honey?"

"No, thanks, Gram."

"Wyatt called again."

"Don't care," Paige said stubbornly.

Mary watched her sadly. "Try to sleep if you can. I'll leave the door propped open, so you can call me if you need me."

She nodded. "Oh, Gram, who's doing the drop tonight?"

"Jeanette is. Dori was supposed to, but well, you know Dori . . . But don't you worry about a thing." Mary patted her arm and then padded softly from the room.

"Gram, crutches!" Paige called after her.

"Oh, all right," she heard her grandmother grumble.

Paige shifted the hot water bottle to a comfortable position on her aching ear. She sighed. Her ear might be feeling slightly better, but her heart certainly wasn't. As she lay in bed, all she could think about was Wyatt's accusations.

How could he profess to love her and think such horrible things about her? Did he really think she was capable of anything so noxious as involvement with drugs?

She closed her eyes, hoping for sleep. Only moments later, she heard Mary in the hallway, talking to Wyatt. "I'm sorry, Wyatt, but she doesn't want to see you."

"Please, Mary, let me in."

"I don't blame her for not wanting to talk to you, Wyatt," Mary said with a disgusted snort. "Wyatt, how could you think . . . ?"

"I know. I know. Don't even say it." From her bedroom, Paige could hear the remorse in his voice. "Please, Mary, I need to talk to Paige."

To Paige's surprise, she heard Mary give him permission to see her. "Don't be long. She's in a lot of pain with that ear."

Gram! Why was Gram allowing Wyatt to see her? Aside from the fact she was furious with him, she looked like death warmed over.

When Wyatt stepped into the room, his blue eyes reflecting concern, she took one look at him and pulled the covers up over her head. "Leave, Wyatt!"

"Paige, we need to talk."

"Oh, I think *you've* said enough."

"I can't blame you for not wanting to talk to me, but please, Paige, you know we have to talk."

"Do not," she said in a muffled voice.

When he sat down on the bed and gently tugged at the blanket covering her head, exposing her feverish face, he winced sympathetically and gently laid a palm on her forehead. "You're burning up."

She extracted his hand from her forehead, and then covered her head with the blanket again. "Wyatt, I don't feel like having visitors. I feel and look terrible. So leave."

"You look fine, but I'm sorry you feel terrible. I guess . . . your ear got worse after . . . well, the other day at the private beach."

This time, she lowered the blanket for a brief few seconds to glare at him. "I told you I had an ear infection before we went down there. And . . . *you*," she said in an accusing tone, "thought I was making it up. Why would I make up an ear infection? Oh, I remember now—to cover up the effects of my illicit drug use."

"When you say it like that, it sounds so awful."

"Oh, I'm sorry. Next time, I'll be sure to sugarcoat it." She yanked the blanket over her face again. "Go, Wyatt!"

"I'm not leaving," he said. "I feel terrible."

"You and me both," she grumbled. "And why are you here again?" She dropped the blanket briefly. "Is this an intervention? Have you come to take me to rehab?"

Wyatt smiled wanly. "Can I consider the fact that you're talking to me at all a good sign?"

She pulled the blanket more securely over her face. "No!" came her muffled response.

"Look, Paige, I know I was wrong. I could tell by your reaction on the beach that I sort of missed the mark . . ."

"You *sort of* missed the mark?"

He tugged the blanket off her face. She tried to wrench it from him, but he held firm. His sincere eyes bored into hers. "Look, I may have been wrong . . ."

When he couldn't say the words, she supplied them for him. "Oh, you *may* have been wrong about me being a *drug trafficker* . . . "

"Could you stop saying that, please?" He smiled hopefully.

"Don't I at least get brownie points for still loving you even when I thought you were . . ."

"A drug trafficker!"

"Stop saying that." He scrubbed a hand over his eyes. "Paige, in my defense, you are up to something. You know it, I know it, and you know I know it." He shook his head ruefully. "What was I supposed to think? You're picking up unmarked boxes at some hole-in-the-wall location, and you won't tell me what's in the boxes—not that it's really any of my business," he acknowledged. "However, you admitted on our drive to Portland that you were involved in something, and asked me to give you time. And Paige, when you mentioned you didn't want me privy to whatever is going on because I'm a cop, well, what was I supposed to think? And then," he said as he raised a finger, "in your sleep, you mentioned having to make a 'drop.' Can you please try to see my point of view? Can you understand why my protective instincts flared?"

"You just want to make an arrest!" she accused. "Yeah, that's right, you want to make the collar. You're looking for the big payday . . ."

"What?" He gave her a puzzled glance. "Yeah, my biggest career aspiration is to arrest my girlfriend . . ."

"I'm not your girlfriend," she insisted angrily, her eyes shooting daggers.

"Are you ever going to forgive me?" he murmured miserably.

Paige rose up in the bed and wrapped her arms around her knees. She sighed loudly, and then winced from a stabbing pain in her ear. "Wyatt, would you please hand me that bottle of pills on the nightstand?"

"Which one?" he asked.

"The one for pain."

He picked one up. "Is it this one?"

She nodded.

He opened the bottle and tipped out a pill. He passed it to her, along with a glass of water beside the bed.

She nodded at the bottle still in his hand. "You might want to have those checked out at the lab."

"Paige, please don't . . ."

She eased back against the pillow, but this time turned to face the opposite direction. She awkwardly propped the hot water bottle over her ear, balancing it on the side of her face.

"I can't see you with the hot water bottle like that," he said.

"That's exactly the point."

"Paige, please talk to me."

"I don't feel like talking, Wyatt. I feel like sleeping. My ear is killing me."

When he lifted the hot water bottle and gently stroked her cheek, she pulled away from him. "Wyatt, do not touch me. I am so furious with you . . ."

In answer, he smoothed his hand across her brow, and then reached for her, pulling her into his arms. "I don't blame you. But you know my heart is in the right place."

She turned toward him for a split second. "I know no such thing."

"Yes, you do."

Suddenly, the radio on his duty belt crackled and a dispatcher began talking. Wyatt turned it up to hear it. "Shoot," he muttered. "Paige, I have to go. There's been a bad accident just north of town. I probably won't get home until late, so I'll be by in the morning to check on you."

"What makes you think I want you to check on me, Wy?"

He smiled. "Because you just called me Wy."

Outside Paige's bedroom, Wyatt called out a thank-you to Mary. When she didn't respond, he quickly ducked into the family room to see if she was in her favorite recliner. She wasn't. When his eyes lit on the boxes stacked in the corner of the room—the boxes he himself had carried into the house— he saw that one sat a foot or two away from the others, and the top was open.

He glanced around. Should he look inside? He didn't have a warrant, he thought, and then smiled sheepishly. Heck, he lived on the property. Besides, if looking inside could help him understand what was going on with Paige, he had to chance it.

He crossed the room and knelt down beside the box. He flipped back a flap, and his mouth dropped open. He studied the contents with a weary smirk on his face, as he scooped up a handful of agates and let them drop through his fingers. Those rocks looked mighty familiar.

He rose with a sigh, and then a smile lit his face ever so briefly. The smile vanished. *Was there really anything to be smiling about?*

He was about to detour to talk to Paige, but stopped short when his radio crackled again, the dispatcher requesting his estimated time of arrival at the accident scene. He'd nearly forgotten the accident. He hated to leave, but he didn't have a choice.

Chapter Seventeen

Mary ran into Paige's bedroom and flipped on the light. "Oh, Paige, honey, I hate to wake you, but please, you have to wake up! Something terrible has happened."

Paige rose, blinking against the onslaught of light. "What—what is it, Gram? Is it Wyatt? Is he hurt?"

"No, no, thank God, it isn't that."

"Is it one of the ladies?"

"No, no, they're fine. Well, I haven't heard from Jeanette yet . . ." She waved off that worry for now. "Oh, honey, try to wake up. I have to show you something. Oh, Paige, it's just awful."

Paige struggled to understand her grandmother, as Mary shoved a piece of paper into her hands. "Honey, read it—hurry."

Paige glanced at the clock beside her bed. "Gram, it's five o'clock in the morning. What's so important that I have to read it right now? And what are you doing up?"

"I always stay awake when you or any of the girls are making

164

the drop. I want to be beside the phone in case something happens."

"Yes, okay, but . . . what's so important about this paper?"

"Oh, honey," she moaned, "I've been so busy with Operation Save Agate Cove, I haven't been paying attention to, well, much else. Just now, as I was waiting for the 'all clear' call from Jeanette, I decided to sort through my junk mail. Anyway, this came . . ." She glanced at the paper in Paige's hands with anguished eyes. "Paige, just read it."

Paige scanned the sheet, her eyes nearly bulging out of her head. She read it a second time, this time more carefully. "Is this a bad dream?" she asked.

"Honey, it's real all right," Mary said. "It's a nightmare."

The letter was dated three days before and came from the *Television Shopping Show.* "Wait, let's recap," Paige said, still struggling to understand. "Gram, this can't be right. The letter says they somehow sent us hundreds of hand-cut gemstones mixed in with one of the boxes of agates." She shook her head. "I don't remember seeing any gemstones, do you?"

Mary shook her head no.

"Okay, they say the gemstones are worth thousands, perhaps more." Paige gulped and met Mary's gaze. "I wonder why they didn't call you. It seems to me they would have called the instant they found the problem."

Mary looked sheepish. "They may have tried. I keep forgetting to plug in my answering machine."

"Oh, Gram. Okay, they go on to say that although the error was theirs, we're obliged to return the gems as quickly as possible—that a reasonable person would have recognized the difference between the agates and the gems. Gram, they're threatening legal action if we don't return them."

"But we don't have them!" Mary cried. "Wait, I'll check through the remaining boxes. Maybe they're there."

"Okay, let's slow down, Gram. We know we didn't drop any gemstones during the last several mornings . . ."

"How can we be sure? We've already gone through a couple of boxes of the ones you and Wyatt picked up in Portland."

"Well, for one thing, we haven't heard happy tourists shouting, 'Eureka!' " Paige quipped.

"And scientists haven't shown up to explain the phenomenon," Mary added.

"Cut gemstones wouldn't bring scientists," Paige said with a sigh. "Maybe treasure hunters or . . . jewelers," she added with a humorless laugh. "Wait, Gram, didn't you open up a new box for this morning's drop?"

Mary nodded, her eyes widened fearfully.

"Okay, okay, did you notice anything different about the agates?"

"No, but Paige, I hardly paid any attention at all to what I was doing. I was in a hurry to get a bag ready for Jeanette, and I just scooped them in. The process has gotten kind of old hat, so I really don't pay much attention anymore."

"So, is it possible Jeanette may have dropped some of the gemstones on the beach this morning?"

Mary looked stricken. "I'll check the box."

She hurried to the family room, ignoring her crutches in order to get there quickly. She knelt down and began sifting through the agates. "I'm not seeing anything out of the ordinary," she told Paige, who had come up behind her.

"That doesn't mean they weren't there. You could have easily scooped up the gemstones if they happened to be in the box. Oh, Gram . . . ," she murmured miserably.

Mary rose to her feet. "I'll call Jeanette."

"Okay, that would probably be good."

Mary dialed her friend, but Jeanette didn't pick up. She tried again, to no avail. "She's not answering. I hope she's all right."

Paige struggled to clear her mind—to figure out what to do next. Her ear began aching again and she wanted nothing more than to go to bed, pull the covers over her head, and hope she would wake up to find this had been a bad dream.

Suddenly, Mary dashed to the coat closet and pulled her coat off a hanger.

"Gram, what are you doing?"

"I'm going down to the public beach. If Jeanette did drop any gemstones down there, I have to find them."

"I'm not letting you go down there," Paige said, aghast. "What if something happens to you?"

"If Jeanette did drop those gemstones on the beach"—she shook her head—"I have to find them."

"I'm going," Paige said in a tone that defied argument.

"You are not! What about your ear?"

"I'll wear an earplug in my infected ear. Gram, I have to go. I know what I'm doing. I'll know where to look."

"You can't go down to that beach wearing an earplug. You won't be able to hear anything. What if a sneaker wave catches you unawares?"

"I'll keep my good ear turned toward the ocean," she assured her.

"Paige, I don't know about this. Even if Jeanette did drop the gemstones, how will you find them all?"

Paige shook her head uncertainly. "I don't know, but I have to try. Gram, this is bad—really bad."

Mary handed her a canister of pepper spray. "Paige, be safe."

As Paige hurried down the sandy trail to the beach, her heart pounded in her chest. If she found a single gemstone on that beach, it meant there could be hundreds spread out in the wet sand. How could she possibly find them all?

She felt sick, beyond the pain of her ear infection. She suddenly wished they had never tried to save the town. Summer was only half-over. If the tourists stopped coming now, everything they had done would be for naught anyway.

Paige knew that if the locals or tourists did happen upon any gemstones in the morning, which seemed a certainty if Jeanette had made a mixed drop of agates and gemstones, then the town would experience a media circus the likes of which they had never seen before, but . . . it would be short-lived.

The authorities would easily track the gemstones to Mary, and then to the rest of them. Not only would they face the music over Operation Save Agate Cove, but they would also have to face the *Television Shopping Show* and their team of lawyers.

Paige felt sicker with each passing moment. How had things gone so bad? Their intentions were good. Surely that counted for something. A feeling of dread descended over her. It didn't matter that their intentions were good. She knew well the old adage—that the road to hell was paved with good intentions.

As she dropped down on her knees to search an area of wet sand, she kept her good ear toward the ocean. The waves were fierce, with weather forecasters predicting a storm to land with ferocity by sunup. If the gemstones were here, she needed to find them fast.

Paige glanced around her, her knees sunk in the sand as she patted all around her. She picked up a stone, studied it, and cast it aside. She glanced around her again, assuring she was alone on the beach, and she turned on her flashlight. She panned across the immediate area, but didn't spot anything remotely resembling a cut gem. She rose and walked a few yards up the shoreline, and then knelt down again.

She did the same routine over and over, but didn't find a single gemstone. Surely that had to be a good sign. Surely it meant that Jeanette hadn't dropped any of the valuable stones onto the beach.

As Paige searched in the wet sand, she heard the mighty roar of the ocean in her good ear, but heard only a faint roar in the bad ear. The earplug, although necessary, created a sound in her ear much like she heard when, as a child, she had pressed a seashell to her ear in order to hear the sound of the ocean.

Paige stood up again, scanning the surf. It seemed to grow angrier by the second, with foamy whitecaps topping each crest. Each thunderous wave that broke on the shore appeared bigger than the one before it. The wind was picking up as well, and Paige realized she needed to get back to her grandmother's house.

She hadn't found a single gemstone, and she had to believe they just weren't here. She realized she had covered about two-thirds of the way to the dune, but decided she just couldn't risk staying out much longer. The sun would be rising soon, and someone could easily spot her on the beach.

With a weary sigh, she turned around and started the trek back to the safety of her grandmother's house. Occasionally, she dropped to her knee to check out a stone with a conspicuous sparkle or color, but, thankfully, none turned out to be gemstones.

When she spotted a particularly large, shiny stone, she bent down and discovered it was an agate rather than a gemstone, but it proved a mistake for her to have stopped. Suddenly, she was slapped by a wave, followed by something harder. It struck at the back of her knees, causing her to collapse like a rag doll in the frigid water.

She began flailing in the water, attempting to get her feet beneath her. Something hard kept coming at her, seemingly relentless in its attack. What was it? She had to get away, and she rose as best she could and tried to fling herself toward the shore.

To her shock, someone suddenly took hold of her and hauled her out of the ocean. With her hair in her face and the earplug in her ear, she had a curious feeling of sensory deprivation. Who held her? The hand on her arm was so strong it had to belong to a man.

Instinctively, she began fighting, and managed to pull away from him. She blindly reached for the pepper spray in her pocket. She aimed it in front of her, taking a threatening stance. Through her wind-whipped hair, she could only vaguely make out a figure in front of her. She thought it was a man, and she thought she heard him say something, but she couldn't make it out. When he caught her arm again, she did what she had to do. She deployed the fiery spray in his direction. The man released her.

Unfortunately, she had fired into the strong winds, and the pepper spray came back into her own face. Her eyes burned intensely and she began coughing. She felt the sting of it on her face and neck, and for a second she considered diving headlong into the ocean to wash it away. But that wasn't an option, since whoever had grabbed her before suddenly did so again.

"It's okay," she heard a distant voice call out.

She realized she had little choice but to trust that voice, but she sincerely doubted that anything was okay.

Paige felt herself half-carried off the beach, across the parking lot, and to a car. She struggled to open her burning eyes, but simply couldn't see a thing. She couldn't stop choking either. It felt as if the pepper spray had seared her throat.

Once she was situated in the car, she felt a firm hand tip her head back and begin dousing her eyes with water. It didn't help much, and soon, she felt herself belted into the seat and driven somewhere.

"Where are we going?" she asked fearfully, but if the man

answered, she didn't hear him. The earplug prevented her from hearing properly, and she was so rattled, it didn't occur to her to remove it.

Suddenly, the car came to an abrupt stop, and she braced herself for what might happen next. She couldn't hear, she couldn't see, and she realized that she was so unsteady on her feet, she couldn't walk. And for all intents and purposes, she felt as if she was on fire. The pain was excruciating, like having fire ants all over her face and neck, even up her nose and down her throat.

"Come on," the voice said loudly.

Paige finally remembered the earplug. She reached up to pull it out of her ear with a trembling hand, and suddenly she could hear again.

"What were you doing out there?" Wyatt's angry voice exploded in her ear, but she couldn't have been happier to hear it.

"Wyatt, is that you?" She reached a hand out, attempting to find him.

He took her by the hand and hauled her into the Agate Cove Jail. Inside, he practically carried her to one of the cots in a cell and instructed her to lie down. He hurried away to retrieve a case of water from behind his desk. One by one, he uncapped the bottles and began dousing her eyes with the water.

The clean, crystal water helped enough that she was finally able to blink her eyes open to see shapes. Wyatt continued pouring the water, until she finally rose up, gasping. "I'm . . . drowning," she said.

"Yeah, you almost did drown, out there on that beach!" he said harshly. "What were you thinking, Paige? You could have been killed."

"I don't know what happened," she said shakily. "I was . . ."

"You were what?" he demanded. When she didn't answer, he said, "You were hit by a log, that's what," he hissed. "And you're lucky to be alive. If I hadn't gone down to that beach after I finished up with that accident . . ." He raked a hand though his hair and began pacing the cell. He finally stopped and aimed a finger at her. "You're going to talk to me, Paige, and you're going to talk to me now."

"Where do you want me to start?" she asked, sitting up, and wincing from the injuries to the back of her legs.

"At the beginning, of course," he told her, folding his arms across his chest. Suddenly, he shook his head as if he had overlooked an important detail. "But first, we have to get you out of those clothes. You're already sick enough."

"I'm fine," she lied.

"You are not." He stormed off, toward the front door, and stopped at the threshold. "Get out of those clothes now. I'll get you something to wear."

He left the building to retrieve a pair of shorts and a T-shirt from a gym bag in his patrol car. When he entered the jail, he found Paige still sitting in her soaking-wet clothing.

"I told you to get out of those wet clothes."

"Not until I have something to change into," she said defiantly.

He passed her the shorts and shirt. "Change your clothes *now!*"

She awkwardly rose and then did a circular gesture with her finger. He rolled his eyes heavenward but turned around.

Getting her soggy, sand- and pepper-spray-covered clothing off wasn't an easy task. Wyatt turned at one point to help her, and she screamed. "Turn around, Wyatt!"

"Good grief, Paige. When we're married . . ."

His words didn't register in her current state of mind. "I mean it, Wyatt. Turn *around*."

He had to admit that he found her modesty endearing.

Finally, Paige sank onto the edge of the cot. "Okay," she murmured. "You can turn around now."

Wyatt turned, and to her surprise, gently hauled her off the cot. The too-big shorts she wore nearly slid down her legs, but she tugged at them until she had gathered the excess material in her hand. Wyatt gently eased her around, wincing when he saw that huge purple bruises had already colored her slim legs. He shook his head furiously, and then surprised her when he pulled her into his arms.

"Paige, you could have been killed."

"I know, Wyatt," she said with a sniffle. "It was stupid."

Suddenly, he thrust her away from him. "Come on." He led her to the dry cot in the other cell, sat her down on it, and then left to retrieve a blanket. This cot was unmade, but he had soaked the blankets on the other one when he had rinsed her eyes with water.

Paige mumbled a thanks for the blanket, and then watched as Wyatt began pacing again, demanding an explanation for her being on the beach. When she opened her mouth to speak, he interrupted her. "So you know," he said loudly, "I know it has to do with the rocks. You know, the ones in Mary's family room, and the ones on the beach."

She glanced up in alarm, her eyes still burning, and now damp from the tears threatening to spill over. "You figured it out," she said resignedly. "I didn't want you to know. Oh, no, I didn't want you involved in this—your career . . ."

His eyes narrowed as understanding dawned. "Paige," he said, taking his voice down a notch, "what were you thinking? You could have been killed out there." His eyes widened in horror. "How many times have you gone out there and thrown those agates on that beach?"

She winced as she did a mental count.

"Okay, okay," he groaned, "enough times to have to think long and hard about it. Okay, talk—tell me everything—from the beginning. Paige, I mean *everything*."

She recounted the story, her heart breaking at the thought

that now Wyatt was drawn into Operation Save Agate Cove, and as a result, would be forced to make some hard decisions. Would he arrest her and Mary, and the others?

When she was done talking, Wyatt dropped onto the cot beside her. "I can't believe Mary got you involved in this," he said angrily.

"Don't blame her, Wyatt," Paige said in a firm voice. "She loves this town. She did it for the town."

"No, *you* did it for the town," he told her. "And it nearly killed you." He raked a hand through his hair, his eyes reflecting his anguish. "Paige, I think about that woman Deputy Harada saw on the beach—the one swept away by the waves. That could have been you. We'll never know what happened to that poor soul."

"Oh . . . she's all right," Paige muttered wanly, without realizing she'd said the words out loud.

Suddenly, Wyatt sprung to his feet. "That was *you?*" he demanded, as he roughly paced the cell. "That was you? Oh, Paige," he exclaimed. He spun around and hauled her to her feet again. He pulled her against him, as she simultaneously made a mad grab for her shorts, lest they drop to her feet.

He held her so tight that she finally muttered, "Wyatt, I can't breathe."

"Then we're even," he said softly, his voice rife with emotion. He finally pulled back to stare into her face, as if to assure himself she was really all right.

"What happens now, Wyatt?" Paige asked. "Are you going to arrest me?" She sat back down on the cot.

"Am I going to *arrest* you?" He shook his head and laughed without humor, and then walked away from her. "Well, on a positive note, at least you're not a drug user."

"And I'm not a drug trafficker," she supplied.

"Can you please not say that again?" he said wearily.

"Okay—but what are you going to do? Wyatt, Gram won't last ten minutes in prison."

He looked taken aback.

"Well, you know, essentially, we committed fraud. We lured tourists here under false pretenses."

Wyatt dropped onto the cot beside her, his face sick with worry. "Let me think." He stroked his jaw. "I guess in a sense it was a hoax, perpetrated on unsuspecting tourists, but the agates are real . . ." He snared her gaze. "They *are* real?"

"As far as I know. Wait, yes, they have to be. Would anyone make a synthetic agate?" She shook her head. "Wait, no, remember, the scientists said they were definitely real agates— well, they didn't say they weren't real agates. But, they don't have the kind of value that other stones might have . . ."

Her words trailed off and she winced. She remembered the missing gemstones. She refrained from telling Wyatt about them now. She just couldn't bring herself to do it quite yet.

"Okay," Wyatt mused, "Mary owned the agates and I guess if she chose to *throw* them away, it was her prerogative. And then, the tourists took ownership of the agates, and they didn't pay for them . . ." He emitted a haggard sigh. "Paige, I have to think about this, and I'm just not thinking very straight right now."

"Wyatt," she said hesitantly, "I'm so sorry about everything. I didn't want you involved in this. I really didn't. It's why I couldn't confide in you. I couldn't risk you losing your job."

He nodded, and then his eyes took on a deer-in-the-headlights kind of stare.

"What is it, Wyatt?" she asked, panic edging her voice as she braced for his answer.

"Paige, I'm involved," he said in measured tones. "Oh, I'm involved, all right."

"You mean, you're involved because I've finally told you."

"No, Paige," he said resignedly, and then did an imitation of a trial lawyer. " 'Miss Kelley, how did you acquire the agates that you distributed over the public beach at Agate Cove?' 'Well, Gram ordered them off of the *Television Shopping Show,* and Undersheriff Hall drove me to Portland to pick them up.' "

Paige looked stricken and fell back against the cinderblock wall of the cell. "Oh, Wyatt, I never thought about that!" She rose to her feet and began pacing, clutching at the excess material at the waistline of the shorts. Wyatt winced when he saw her legs, which were now black with bruising.

"Paige, sit down. We'll . . . figure this out."

"Wyatt, just shoot me now," she muttered.

"There will be no shooting today," a firm voice said from the doorway.

Wyatt and Paige glanced toward the voice and saw Jeanette standing at the threshold. She strode into the jail, followed by Minnie, Dori, and Mary, who looked absolutely sick.

The women suddenly nodded in unison, and then struck their arms out. "Cuff us, copper," Jeanette said. "We did the crime, and we're prepared to do the time." She glanced at Paige. "The girl is innocent."

"What happened to the girl?" Mary cried, her voice sounding near hysterical. "I mean, Paige, what happened to you, honey? Jeanette saw Wyatt arrest you and drag you here, but honey, just look at you."

"It's a long story, Gram," she said tiredly. "But Wyatt didn't arrest me—at least, not yet."

Wyatt rose from the cot. "Ladies," he said in a menacing tone, "I'm so glad you're here. Unfortunately, I have to leave. I have to take Paige to see a doctor." He raised a warning finger. "But when I get back here, I'd better find each and every one of you here and waiting to talk to me. Do we understand one another?"

"May I go with you to take Paige to the doctor's?" Mary asked, a worried frown marring her brow.

"I'm afraid not," Wyatt said.

"I don't know, girls," Jeanette said, glaring at Wyatt with hands on her hips. "He doesn't scare me. I say we don't tell him anything. I say, between the five of us, we can easily take him. He won't shoot us," she said confidently. "We'll use Paige to block us. He won't risk Paige."

"Jeanette!" Mary cried with a gasp. "She's my grand-daughter!"

"Jeanette, that's enough out of you," Wyatt warned. "Look, Paige has already told me everything," he said, but then was quick to point out, for her sake, that he had already figured things out.

As he led Paige out of the jail, he called over his shoulder. "Ladies, don't even think about making a break for it. I'll be calling the road crew to assure that none of you attempts to escape Agate Cove via the only way out of Agate Cove right now."

"The detour!" they said in unison.

"Dagnabbit!" Jeanette cried.

Chapter Eighteen

After stopping by the medical clinic and learning that Paige hadn't sustained any broken bones from being struck by the log, Wyatt asked the doctor to have another look at her ear. The doctor immediately prescribed ear drops, to be used in conjunction with the antibiotics, and promised that Paige truly would be on the mend soon.

On the drive to Mary's house, both rode in silence. Paige noticed that Wyatt white-knuckled the steering wheel, and she knew she had much to do with his stiff posture.

She had dragged him into something that could potentially affect his life and career. If only she hadn't been down on that beach, searching for the gemstones that weren't even there. She nearly groaned aloud at the thought of those gemstones, and the prospect that she would have to tell Wyatt about them sooner rather than later.

When she got back home, she would need to sort through each and every remaining box. If the gemstones were there, she would find them. No matter that she wanted to go to sleep, that her body ached, that her eyes burned, and that her ear throbbed. She had to find those gemstones, because if she didn't find them, Gram would definitely go to jail.

On top of everything else, she and the ladies were now forced to abandon Operation Save Agate Cove, and she was certain the town would suffer for it. She sighed heavily, and Wyatt turned toward her briefly.

"I still can't believe Mary drew you into her scheme."

"She had to," Paige said in her grandmother's defense. "With her foot broken, she couldn't make the drops."

"Make the drops." He repeated the words with a crisp shake of his head. "Paige . . . ," he groaned.

"Wyatt, I'm sorry, but I couldn't tell her no. She's done so much for me. Until I was sixteen years old, I didn't even know she existed, or she me, but look at us. We couldn't be closer if I had known her my whole life. Wyatt, I adore her."

"I know. I do too. However, I'm not particularly fond of Jeanette. Maybe I'll throw the book at her," he said, taking a stab at humor.

"We've put you in a tough spot," she observed sadly.

"Between a rock and a hard place," he said with a sigh, and then laughed at his joke.

Paige laughed too, pretending she and Mary hadn't made the same joke many times over the past several weeks. "Are we going to jail?" Paige asked, fearing his answer.

"Not if I can help it," he told her, "not if I can help it."

Inside her grandmother's house, Paige took a shower, while Wyatt went to his apartment to do the same.

Done with her shower, Paige dressed in comfortable sweats, and then retrieved a blanket from her bedroom. She couldn't seem to warm up, and unfortunately, her eyes and throat still stung from the pepper spray. She wondered how long the discomfort would last.

She headed toward the family room, and spied her grand-mother's answering machine light blinking, indicating a message waiting. She was relieved to see Mary had finally turned it on. She pressed PLAY, and then nearly collapsed with relief. The *Television Shopping Show* had found the missing gemstones. "We're so sorry if we caused you any unnecessary inconvenience," an overly cheerful woman's voice said.

"Yeah, you and me both," Paige muttered aloud.

Thankfully, Mary was off the hook for the gemstones. Now, it remained to be seen what Wyatt intended to do about everything else.

When he strode into Mary's house, he found Paige on the sofa, curled up in the blanket. She was still shaking from both cold and relief. Wyatt dropped onto the couch beside her and pulled her against him, wrapping her in his arms. "Better?" he asked.

She met his gaze, a hesitant expression in her eyes. "What happens next, Wyatt?" she asked fearfully.

"Well, for one thing, I think you'd better marry me, otherwise there's no telling what might happen to you next. You're hanging out with a questionable crowd these days."

Paige gasped. "Wyatt, are you joking?"

"No way—they are questionable."

"I mean . . . about your wanting to marry me?"

"Why would I joke about marriage?" he asked. "I've been waiting ten years to marry you. I think I've waited long enough, don't you?"

Paige was speechless. What could she say?

"Well?" he prompted.

"But, Wyatt, you can't marry me. I'm a criminal."

He laughed out loud and shook his head. "The more I think about this Operation Save Agate Cove business, the more I think we'd better keep it to ourselves—and I mean, *keep it to ourselves.* Do you think we can count on the ladies to keep their mouths shut?"

"But Wyatt, aren't you obliged to arrest us? Aren't we lawbreakers?"

"Ah, Paige, it's not as if you bilked the tourists out of their money. Sure, you lured them here using the agates." He searched her face. "But Mary paid for them. Like I said before, if she wanted to give them away, it was her choice."

"Really?" she said hopefully.

"And you ladies distributed so many that, near as I can tell, everyone left here happy. No, honey, I think we'll just let it go." He raised a warning finger. "But the agate drops have got to stop. It's not safe for anyone to be down on that beach alone in the early-morning hours. I still cringe when I think . . ."

She knew he was referring to her being swept out to sea by a sneaker wave. He pulled her close. "Will you marry me, Paige?"

She felt the tears spring to her eyes. "You're sure you still want me?"

"I always have, Paige." He smoothed the hair off her brow and searched her eyes. "We ended up traveling different roads for a while." He flashed a quick grin. "We took a detour, if you will. But I think it's fate that our paths intersected again. I don't know how I've gotten along without you, sweetheart. I definitely don't know how you've gotten along without me," he teased.

He kissed her, lovingly and tenderly, and she knew then that she had come home. She sighed contently, but then gasped.

"Wy, one thing. What about the ladies? We left them at the jail. We really can't leave them there all day."

"I'm absolutely confident that Jeanette will stage a jailbreak. No worries, honey—no worries," he said, and then their lips merged in another kiss.

Epilogue

W_{yatt} Hall!" Jeanette snapped, "who do you think you are?"

"I think I'm the undersheriff of this county, and potentially your arresting officer if you don't stop griping and do what I say. If you don't, Jeanette, you will be spending time behind bars."

"But look at all that litter," she groaned. "This town and the beach are still a mess after the Fourth of July party."

"Yes, and you're going to help clean it up. Here, take your litter stick."

"I didn't make the mess," Jeanette complained, but she finally accepted the litter stick from him.

Wyatt glanced at Paige, who stood nearby, watching the exchange between him and Jeanette with a ghost of a smile on her face. When Wyatt indicated Jeanette with a nod and rolled his eyes, Paige chuckled.

"Why is Paige off the hook?" Jeanette demanded. "It doesn't seem fair, if you ask me."

"I'm not asking you, and besides, Paige has suffered

enough," he said crisply. "And frankly, I don't want her spending time with you and your friends. You're all a very bad influence on her. How can you live with yourselves? Bringing her to this town and introducing her to a life of crime—you should know better."

"Come on over here and I'll show you a bad influence, Wyatt Hall," Jeanette said in a flirtatious tone.

Wyatt glared at her. "Look, Jeanette, out of respect for my future wife, you will cease and desist with the suggestive comments."

Suddenly, Jeanette broke out in a wide grin, as did Minnie and Dori. Mary, who hurried forward to throw her arms around Paige, also beamed. "Oh, honey, congratulations," she said.

"Thanks, Gram." Paige extended her left hand and fluttered her ring finger, showing off the diamond.

"It's beautiful," Mary said, and the ladies echoed their agreement.

Jeanette's goodwill proved short-lived. "Are you sure you want to wake up to that face every morning?" she asked Paige, hitching a thumb at Wyatt. "He ain't gonna look like that forever."

"I'm absolutely sure," Paige said with a chuckle.

"What does your father have to say about this engagement?" Jeanette asked. "My guess is he won't approve."

"Dad couldn't be happier for me. In fact, he's coming to visit this weekend."

"Oh," Jeanette said cheerfully, "you will bring him by the diner to say hello?"

Wyatt clasped his hands together. "Okay, ladies, let's get this show on the road. Your litter is waiting." He turned to Mary. "I think you'd better handle the parking lot. With your foot, I don't want you walking on that uneven sand. You might injure it again."

"Oh, sure, you're already showing favoritism for your future grandmother-in-law," Jeanette accused. "Come on, Wyatt, it's windy out here. And I have work to do at the diner. Besides, my foot hurts too."

"Your foot is fine, and you should have thought of all of that before you turned to a life of crime. Jeanette, I don't hear the other ladies complaining about litter duty," he said reasonably. "And I should think you'd be counting your lucky stars. I only fined you for littering and didn't charge you with anything else. I can sure tack on other charges if you'd like."

"Littering, ha!—how can our agate drops be called littering?" she demanded. "Agates are natural! They come from the earth. How's that littering?"

"If you'd like me to take a second look at this matter, I will," he warned. "And if you don't get out there and do your job, I'll send you out next time in neon orange coveralls labeled 'Offender' on the back. Then you'll have some explaining to do to your customers."

"You wouldn't!"

"Try me!"

Jeanette glanced at Mary. "Why don't you evict him?"

"Evict me? I'm moving in permanently," Wyatt told her, a wicked gleam in his eye.

Jeanette's jaw dropped, and then, with a final mock-angry glance at Wyatt, she headed out to the sand. The other ladies followed, while Mary went to the parking lot.

Wyatt sat down on a bench alongside the beach and patted the space beside him. Paige sat down, and he draped an arm around her and pulled her close. He extended his other arm along the back of the bench and crossed his legs in front of him. He looked like a king surveying his kingdom.

"How's your ear?" he asked Paige, tipping his head to kiss her on the cheek.

They all glanced up at Mary. "No!" they said in unison. "She's definitely learned her lesson."

"Looks like Mother Nature has come to the rescue of our town," Wyatt observed, "and Agate Cove will live to see another day. Okay, ladies, get back to work."

Back at the bench, Paige snared Wyatt's gaze. "Wy," she said, "did I just see what I thought I did? Those agates are beautiful. They're even more beautiful than the ones Gram bought from the *Television Shopping Show.*"

He responded by draping an arm over her shoulder and pulling her close. He kissed her, and then, together, they watched the breaking waves.

"Oh, did I mention that the roads opened today?" Wyatt said.

Paige turned toward him. "No more detour?" she said.

He shook his head. "No more detour," he confirmed.

"Not that I'm going anywhere," she said, smiling into his ocean-blue eyes.

His eyes sparkled when he answered. "Glad to hear it," he said. And then he kissed her.

"It's fine, thank you."

He turned to grin at her. "Life's good, honey," he said. "Just look at that ocean."

"It's stunning."

"It's not as stunning as you are."

She smiled and shook her head. "Ah, thank you. Hey, Wy?"

"Yeah?"

"I'm thinking it's a good thing that Jeanette has apparently forgotten you drove with me to Portland to pick up those agates."

He raised a finger to his lips, and nodded in understanding. "I know. She'd definitely use it against me in a court of law. So, Paige, let's remain silent."

She smiled. "I will."

Wyatt sat back against the bench again, a contented smile on his face. "Hey, what are those ladies doing?" he asked, squinting to see. "Oh, honey," he grumbled, "we'd better check it out. I'm afraid Jeanette's going to make a run for it."

Wyatt took Paige's hand as they walked together to where Jeanette, Minnie, and Dori stood in the wet sand. Mary, who was cleaning up the lot, noticed, and paused to shade her eyes with her hand for a look at whatever was happening on the beach.

"What's up, ladies?" Wyatt called out as he approached. When they reached the women, he raised a questioning brow.

Jeanette aimed a finger at the sand. "Look at that!"

To his surprise and Paige's, the wet sand was littered with beautiful agates of every shape, size, and color.

Wyatt swallowed hard and glanced at each of the women, one at a time. "Not me, not me, wasn't me," they said respectively.

Wyatt glanced at Paige. "Don't look at me. I've learned my lesson," she assured him.